WEED IN GOD'S GARDEN

By

Nagie Monei

* * *

CHAPTER ONE

Life

I wake up to the sun shining through broken and bent blinds. What was once hidden away in the darkness of my room has come to light and I scour at the sight of filth.

A mound of dirty laundry my mother has yet to start greets me with winkled smiles from each garment. There's a foul odor that's lingering in the air as if I stepped in dog shit, vomit, or rotting trash that's mixing in with my own body odor. I walked in last night from the bar to my car and from my car to my bedroom without removing my shoes. Where I stepped in something disgusting? I have no clue. I was intoxicated. Just like the days of my youth minus this massive headache serving as a reminder that I'm too old to be doing this.

I shift my eyes from my worn-out shoes stained with black stuff marks and torn up shoestrings to an old Pink Floyd poster in the corner of my room.

Oh, the good old days when I aspired to be just as big as them in my own group. I had some good times though.

Cruising the twilight streets with my buddies after a grand performance. The wide eyes gaze of adornment from chicks in the crowd and backstage cuddle sessions from a few lucky ones who casually greeted themselves. The constant drug fueled parties we attended each time with a different date.

I wonder what would have become of my life had I committed myself to my dreams of being a lead singer and guitarist and not took it as a simple hobby. I had the looks, attitude, and with a little more persistence on growing my abilities towards playing a guitar I could have been famous...or at least something more of what I am today.

The most shows I played were six and just when my group, Slack Boyz, were starting to make a name for us, *life* happened.

I turn over on my side and feel a snap of a spring under the mattress right near my ankle. I really need to get a new bed. Bigger than this twin sized piece of shit. Someday I will. Probably when I move out, until then, it's small enough to give me some walking space in my bedroom.

The deteriorating antique dresser is taking up majority of the area along with crap that's on the stained carpet. I'll get a bigger place. An apartment maybe. Two bedrooms. One for sleeping and the other for playtime.

"I'm thinking about making it a home theater or a gaming room. What do you think?" I hear myself say to the lucky broad who may enter my life in the future.

She would throw her arms around my neck and pull her body close to mine. *"You should make it a room for all of your nasty behavior."*

"That's what the bedroom is for."

"In this one you can have the toys and whips on display."

I close my eyes feeling my body warm at the thought of a woman' touch. Honestly, I haven't felt one in decades. The soft texture of her hair and skin. The warm lavender scent of her flesh. The cotton candy taste of her lips and the hot sensation of her inner core from her heart to her moist, fruity area.

Releasing a huff of frustration, I roll from my bed onto the floor and dig under my bed for a box. I rarely take it out. Most of the time I sit in my room staring at the watermark-stained ceiling until my mind conjures up something or read a playboy magazine. Today I need visualization to satisfy this urge.

The box holds five x rated flicks. Scanning through each of ones' covers and reading the back for the descriptions, I try to remember my favorite scene in on each tape to be sure I'm picking the best one that would finish the job fast. I can hear my parents stirring about outside of my room. Time of the essence before I'm disturbed and taken from this heavenly feeling.

I don't have a preference when it comes to women. Anyone is fine as long as they do some crazy stunts in the bedroom.

I pick the flick that focuses on the art of lovemaking through quick storytelling and blush at the woman holding her partner close to her chest on the cover.

What is this shameful feeling? I'm hesitant on putting the tape into the VCR connected to the tiny box television, but I have to get this out of my system. My mind is being bombarded with flashbacks of my own acts of intimacy with women whom I adored for ages and admired for mere seconds. Their lightly salted taste, the sweet words they whispered back to me between grunts and moans. Their warmth engulfing every part of my body as my skin fuses with theirs. I imagine myself the lucky man on the screen peeling away his partners undergarments and smile.

"Gene!" My bedroom door is thrown open just as I'm about to finish.

My hand on my privates, I yelp in fright seeing my mother, Carol. She doesn't seem shocked at all with my actions. Instead, she stands there with one hand on the doorknob and the other on her hip. She has a frown smeared on her face as she shakes her head.

"No wonder you didn't hear me callin' you." She says.

I yank my hand out of my boxers and throw a dirty flannel shirt over the television. Thank God the volume was low.

"Damn. Ever heard of knocking?" I snap.

"I did knock." My mother hit my door with her knuckles. Once. Even if I heard her, I'd assume she bumped into the door.

I look at her for a moment until embarrassment washes from my face and fold my legs to cover the lingering stiffness. "Then that should tell you I don't want to be bothered if I didn't say anything."

Carol waves off the notion. "Oh please. You act like I don't know what a grown-

"Ma!" I have to stop her before she humiliates me even further. "What do you want?"

"Can you make a quick run to Jerry's for me?"

I check the time on my table clock. It's going on nine. Not that I'm worried if Jerry is awake or not. He's a dealer so he's always available in some way. It's just that I'm not quite ready to leave my bedroom yet. Nothing could be worse for a guy than going out of the house with two rocks in the sack.

I shoot my mother an annoyed look and she catches it.

"You don't have to go now." She says as she starts to shut the door. "But hurry up."

The thought of my mother casually waiting on me to finish thumping off plus *seeing* her, shot down my mood like a pianist fumbling the last dramatic note just by hearing a cough.

I stand up to the pile of old clothes, grab a clean enough smelling shirt, jeans and head to the shower. Maybe something magical will happen there.

CHAPTER TWO

Family

"Why don't we go over there and start whooping ass!" I hear my father shout as I come out of the bathroom. "We're a grand country. First world. Now our leaders are acting like pussies against these third world roaches."

I stroll past my father without making eye contact but feel his gaze burning against the side of my head like a laser.

Normally I get up in the afternoon. If not for my mother, I'd still be in bed with a little weight lifted off my body. At least mentally equipped to deal with his nonsense targeted towards me or hearing the undertone of his rants at the twenty-four-hour news broadcasting.

Standing in the kitchen, Carol lights a cigarette over a pot of boiling water. She nods her head as my father, Roger continues on with his rant and I wonder if she agrees with him like she has the same prejudice thoughts in mind or she's just motioning in agreement to shut him up from further strife. Either way, once he sees that she is "listening" to him from where he sits, he shuts up and continues to watch the weatherman discussing oncoming showers for the next three days.

The downpour will be great for the sycamores of Greenwood, Montana, making them stronger for next year's furniture creations.

I walk into the living room and throw my leather jacket on a beaten sofa. My father sees me and scoffs.

"Well look who rose from the dead." He says with spit flinging out of his mouth. "My son. My boy. My only good for nothing sack of-

"Good morning to you too, Roger." I say.

"That's Lieutenant Collens, boy. If you aint gonna address me as you father, address me properly! I aint survive Vietnam to be degraded by a piece of lag like yourself."

I keep my lips tight together as my tongue brushes up against the back of my front teeth. The urge to cut deep into his statement is strong but due to his condition, I don't want to bring him down any further. Plus, he is right. I wonder what his attitude be towards me if I did join the military at the ripe age of eighteen like him and served. Would there be a glint of pride in his only son? Would he boast about me to his fellow comrades during the military luncheon at the buffet?

"You got fatter, huh?" Roger questions and chuckles. "Losing more hair. Not gonna get a woman or a job lookin' like that."

"Yeah. Whatever." I bounce up from the sofa and step into the kitchen.

Carol puts out her cigarette on an ashtray made from aluminum foil, takes her pack of smokes from the counter, and stuffs them in the front pouch of her fanny pack. She then tosses two eggs into the hot water and opens a cabinet to pull out a five-day pill container.

I read the label on the orange bottle full of large pills. It's prescribed to her, joint medication for her arthritis.

Gently placing the container down, I examine my mother at the corner of my eyes. She's muttering something other than the days of the week as she drops five pills into each tiny box and listening to her carefully, I only pick up "currency exchange" "check" 'groceries".

She's doing it all. Cleaning, cooking, taking care of Roger and running errands when he's resting. A friend of hers from Bingo comes around to drive her anywhere she needs like a taxi. Why not me? Well, I'm supposed to be looking for a job, apartment, anything that would propel me forward in life. The only errands I run for her are to pick up a bag of weed.

I reach my hand forward and tap her spectacles dangling from a gold beaded rope. "New chain?"

She shows me a gappy smile and fashions her new accessory. "Yeah. Just came in the mail." The chain sways back and forth against the side of her face. "You like?"

My mother was once a beauty. She had a face that was perfected by stunning symmetry and wide sapphire eyes, long, thick natural red hair that stopped at the center of her back, and skin that resembled a porcelain doll straight from the pack.

She used to be a ballerina and a master of the art that later blessed her with opportunities like modeling gigs and a few commercials for her slender body. Once she got married and had me, those dancing days came to a halt. Now, she has black duffle bags under her eyes that are becoming darker each day of her life. They are a sign of her stress, mentally and physically from holding down the fort of the house plus working to keep her own well-being above water. She dyed her red hair blonde because Roger likes blondes, but it made her hair weak and wire looking. As for her doll-like skin, it's still the same, but horribly aged like decorative crape paper no thanks to the speeding process of chain smoking.

She's sixty-two.

I put the cause of her decline of health on my father. Everything was fine while he was stationed overseas. Granted he was fighting in a war, but I'm certain with his bigoted nature he was happy behind the trigger. It was just me and her in the house in a state of content. I remember and miss the days I would find her dancing in the living room to classical tunes and symphonies as if I was looking at glimpse of the former life she let go of due to two life altering decisions.

Now Rogers home permanently and paralyzed from the waist down. It was an accidental shooting from one of his comrades in the spine that left her to take care of him and him to feel like half a man.

I sometimes feel that I am part of her stress as well. I wasn't doing shit then, but it was OK because I was keeping her company.

Now there's two useless men in the house. I should've gotten a job or started my career a long time ago. Anything to take the some of the load from her shoulders. I never tried though. No applications. Didn't bother asking the workers at local diners and convenient stores if they were hiring. I don't even have a high school diploma.

With all of that being pondered, I smile back at my mom and tell her she's a beauty and will forever be one.

"What have you got planned for today?" She asks.

I shrug. "Probably go out and look for a job."

Her eyes light up.

"Oh yeah? Got any ideas on where you wanna work?"

"Anything is fine with me." I say and open the refrigerator. I fix myself a glass of orange juice and chug it down. Just as my mom is about to speak, Roger shouts her name. She starts to walk toward him, but I grab onto her arm. "Ignore him. All he wants to do is see what we are talking about."

"Carol. Goddammit! You hear me?"

My mother huffs and frees her arm from my grasp. "He needs his medicine and is probably hungry."

She prepares his breakfast that consists of two boiled eggs sliced in half, three strips of bacon, a bowl of mixed fruit, and the rest of the orange juice with his medicine. I follow her out of the kitchen and watch her set up a tv dinner stand in front of his wheelchair. While she is doing her caretaker work, Roger glares at me.

I sit on the sofa keeping my eyes locked onto his but notice his body is shaking hard. I guess it's a symptom of his paralysis. Every so often his limp legs shake as if they are trying to come back to life. It angers him that he can't move anymore the way he used to. He can't even chase me out of the house. All he can do is curse me. I laugh at him for being the way he is and unable to work on the thrilling battle grounds. One less trigger-happy fanatic molded that way due to consuming one side of an argument day in and day out.

As the convulsions slow once he takes his medicine, Roger turns his head toward the tv. The reporter says something that sparks his interest. I continue to stare at him. We are not different at all. Both of us are balding, large in the belly, and useless sons of bitches. He looks back at me.

"What the hell are you lookin' at?"

"Nothing much." I say and pick a small piece of cat hair from my jeans.

He takes the rest of his pills and gulps down the orange juice. "Don't you got something to do?"

"I'm watching tv aren't I?"

Carol scurries back into the kitchen. She hates being caught between the two of us while we are fighting since my father always manages to drag her into the argument by questioning her leniency on me now and when I was a kid. She should have made me a tougher man instead of constantly nurturing me. But that was his fucking job.

"Haven't you watched enough?" Roger shuts off the tv just as a news reporter starts talking about an incident involving a person named Lyra hitting my town last year. "Go do something with your life."

"I'm waiting." I mumble.

"For what? Somethin' to fall into your lap?"

"You think I like sitting here with you?"

"I don't give a fuck what you like, boy." Chewed eggs fly out of Rogers mouth as he speaks. "Until you bring in some income in this house, I don't want you sitting here with me. Your presence near me feels like I'm sitting in a monkey's cage."

I stand up with my fist clenched. He wheels backwards away from his breakfast tray and tightens up his hands like he is ready to fight if I swing at him. I won't give him the satisfaction of being a punching bag to release his pent out anger. His weak throws will make me laugh anyways. But I do have some words for him.

"What the hell is your problem?" I ask.

"You!" He shouts back. "You being here is my fucking problem. You lowlife little shit."

I stomp toward him. He raises his fist in the air, but I grab onto his wrist and pin them down between his frail thin legs.

My father knows I'm stronger than him and capable of flipping him out of his wheelchair. Now that I have a grip on him, he's cowering like a scared dog.

"The apple doesn't fall far from the tree." I say and tighten my grasp. Rogers eyes grow wide in panic. He wants to call out for his servant, but to display weakness in the face of his subordinate is damn near a crime to him.

Suddenly, I feel a grip on my shoulder. Carol pulls me back. I release my father and shove him hard.

"Baby." My mother pushes me away from Roger with one hand and digs into her fanny pack with the other. She pulls out wadded money and places it in my hand. "Go to Jerry's and pick me up a bag."

I gaze into her watering blood-shot eyes. She wants me to leave the house so Roger can cool down.

Sighing, I put the money into my pocket and call my father an asshole as I'm leaving through the front door.

CHAPTER THREE

Hit

The car door growls when I open it. It was originally my father's car, bought after he returned from Vietnam and although he was paralyzed long before he made the purchase, I think he got it because there was a sliver of hope doctors would find some cure to his ailment or an engineer to invent a function that would allow him to drive it without the use of his legs. Neither came about and my mother urged him to let me drive it.

It's another reason why he's disappointed in me. I didn't earn a car out of hard work behind discipline. It was given to me in hopes that I'd be able to find a job outside of Greenwood. Maybe somewhere in the city behind a desk wearing a suit. I can't imagine myself doing that type of shit work. The endless cycle of paperwork and meetings bores me to madness.

I climb inside and stick the key into the ignition. It takes a while for the engine to turn over but once it kicks on, the radio set to my favorite rock station plays a familiar song and the air condition hits me with an icy blast. I know my father is seething hearing the car crank and rattle from the living room.

An orangish-yellow lamp dripping oil symbol lightens beside the speedometer and radiates as if faintly calling out to me for help. I have to get an oil change as soon as possible. It's been a year and some months since I washed and serviced the vehicle. It putters as I drive and sometimes refuses to start. All I need is money to fall out of the sky at its clearest even though the forecast said it was going to rain.

I turn off the ac and roll down the window to take in some of the fresh air Montana has to offer thanks to the large pine trees that engulf the state and allow my body to relax in the scenery.

There isn't anything special about my hometown and absolutely nothing has changed about it since I was born in the hospital. If you're coming from out of town through the highway that turns into the main road, you'd be in and out of Greenwood within an hour and a half, only passing one neighborhood that turns off into its own street after you pass the super gas station. From there you'll pass a few car shops, a storage center that holds just about the entire city population's shit, one fast food joint that's overrun with teens and the late generation who refuse to retire. Walking in it, you'd be able to feel the generational tension.

Theres also an old family-owned fishing and gardening store that sometimes has a *For Hire* sign on the window, but the last time I asked for a job, the current employee was cursing out the owner's daughter for constantly breathing down his neck as if he was going to steal bait and I don't have the patience for micro-managing.

The only feasible job to get in this town is to be an arborist. There are enough trees to keep me employed for the rest of my life, granted my out of shape body will allow it.

I sigh and rub my tired eyes. That's all there is out here. Damn near nothing and trees. Finding a job out in the city would mean I'd have to travel two hours every day just to get to and from it.

Carol gave me some extra money, and I think about skipping out of town on the spare funds once I drop off her package. I just want to get away, far as possible to wherever the road stops at a dead end. There I'd begin a new life under an obscure identity. Eventually I would return home to pick up my belongings, but hell, my old shit isn't worth anything. I could do with leaving it behind for the trash.

You think something is going to fall into your lap? Roger's words in his scornful tone are etched in my mind. He says that so often it replays like a scratched record, coming to me whenever I think of life beyond what I already have. I wish a woman, and a job would easily come to me like how his car keys feel into the palm of my hand. However, I like to keep my expectations on everything as simple as possible and hope to see a "hiring now" sign in a window of some place and they would pick me up on the spot so other than that mom-and-pop shop.

The driver behind me honks and I gently raise my foot off the brakes to move slightly further, but not too close to the ass of the car in front of me. Dozens of vehicles ahead, I see the street light lingering on red even though the road is considered a state highway and should always be clear. There are so many people crammed in Greenwood attempting to get out of town and on the turnpike before clock in time but only a fool would decide not to leave thirty minutes early. I'm in no hurry. Better outside than indoors. But Carol and her package. She's going to want it before noon.

"Fuck." I mumble and turn into the mid-town gas station that is gradually deteriorating over time.

Rusted pumps with chipping white paint and at night only two of the neon lights work out of the rest, glowing a bright green AS. Ever since the super stop opened with hot meals included from finer cooks and selections, no one who isn't desperate for gas stops here unless they need a quick pack of condoms, cigs, or stomach knotting hot dogs that've been turning for three days straight.

I rush to the pay phone and tap my pockets. Shit. I don't have change, and I don't think I have any quarters in the car. All I have is a crumpled dollar stained with something brown.

A woman wearing a floral dress, clutching her handbag close to her large chest passes me.

"Excuse me. I'm sorry. Do you have change?"

She smiles, opens a small slot in her purse and pulls out two quarters. "Keep your dollar."

I smile back. She's very pretty, pale skinned, green eyes and red hair with one lock that drapes over her shoulder and like the tip of a curious finger, sits on the top of her breast lightly moving back and forth.

"Why don't you write your number on it?" I say extending the bill her way.

The woman's smile immediately turns down, her nose crunches, and she walks away, dress flowing in the light wind and giving me just a peak at where her thigh meets her buttocks. Well, excuse me. I watch her quickly dash in heels back to her car and pull out of the driveway.

Women.

I call Jerry and another woman answers the phone.

"Bright and Bubblies Cleaning Service."

"Hey, I'll be there in forty-five."

"Wrong number. Moron!"

The phone clicks.

Back in my car, I lean my head out of the window to see how long the traffic is. About twenty-five cars, including mine, are waiting for a stoplight to change, but past that stoplight there's another long line of cars. I don't know how long my mother is willing to wait and put up with Roger's crap on a sober mind, so I get out of the line and turn the car around to take the back roads through the forest. It should get me to my destination unfortunately with added time, but I could use nature's decor of green to bring me a sense of clarity.

The single two-way street is empty. I only pass three cars. Damn, it feels so nice outside. The fresh pine air fills my lungs making it easy for me to breathe and rock out to a song playing on the radio. I have a feeling today is going to be a good day. It's early in the morning, no rain, my spirit feels as if it's resting on a cloud despite the shit I have going on back home. Nothing can bring me down unless I allow it and as long as I remain outside, I'm fine.

Maybe I will travel to the city and look for a job if it means going through the forest to get to the work site every day. It'd be good for my mind to think in a sea of green as long as I got good music and a strong cup of coffee.

Survival and self-restoration will be a breeze, rough the first couple of months being rooted in my home-grown ways, but with a little time to build endurance I may have a chance to change my life.

I take a second to lean over to the passenger's side and scan three cassette tapes on the seat. When I find my favorite, I read the label. A mix of recorded songs from the rock station. Like icing on a cake.

"OH SHIT!"

A face staring back at me and wide black eyes sends a jolt from my stomach and stops right underneath my ribcage to stab me in the lungs. I gasp, slam on the brakes, and yank the wheel to the left, but it's too late. Like a rumble of an oncoming thunderstorm right over my head, the body of a heavy person then slams down on the hood of my trunk, dipping my car low. The smell of burning rubber seeps through the vents and tickles the hairs of my nose.

Oh, my God. I hit someone with my car.

I put my trembling hands back on the steering wheel, tempted to drive away, but I can't put my foot on the peddle or take my eyes off of the body in the side view mirror. It's not moving. I need to see some movement for my consciousness to free me of this guilt that I'm feeling. I'm cool with driving away knowing the person was just injured, but I don't think I can drive away knowing they're dead. Strange? Yeah, I know.

I wait for five minutes. No cars pass by, and the person has yet to move. My mind screams *"DRIVE"* but my heart is telling me otherwise. I keep the car running and get out almost stepping on a black bag. Slowly, I walk to the body and pray it moves an arm or a leg. Something!

Now that I'm closer, I see that I hit a guy. A muscular one at that. He isn't wearing a shirt. Just shorts with an odd pair of sandals that look to have been made from sticks and leaves weaved together. His right leg has been bent out of proportion to where his ankle is at the top of his nape and there's a small puddle of extremely bright blood leaking from his skull. I lightly tap him with the toe of my shoe, but he doesn't move.

"Oh, God." I whisper. I killed someone.

The thought brings on a new wave of anxiety and sadness to my soul as if someone just ripped out my heart and threw my brain in a cyclone. I don't know what to think or do. Fuck! I can't bring this shit home to my parents. My mother would die on the spot under the rage of my father.

I have to get away before a car drives by.

I start to run, but something snags hold of the end of my jeans.

"Holy shit!" I scream and yank myself free.

With a hand coated in blood, the guy reaches up toward me and huffs out the words, "please."

I stand there mouth agape, in total shock and slightly pissed he didn't move before while I was in my car. At least I could've driven off in peace.

Fuck. I can't leave him here like this. I grab a fist full of what hair I have left on the sides of my head and release a growl. I have to take this man to the hospital, but everything will be put on me. I'll be in serious trouble. Yet, I'd rather give my parents this angle of the situation over the worse.

"Fuck! Dammit!" My voice echoes throughout the streets mimicking my frustration as if mocking me. The guy has enough strength to drag himself closer to me and grabs onto my leg with both arms.

"Help me, please."

"Alright." I cry and lift him up. He uses some of his strength to help and bounce on one leg while I hear shattered bones crack. A swift thought hits me along with perplexity towards this guy being able to walk with a twisted leg and a bleeding scalp. *Who the fuck is this?* I've never seen him in town.

I start to pull the man towards my car, but he leans

toward a different direction making it harder on me. He's heavy, twice my size in muscle weight and height.

"What the fuck are you doing?" I yell.

"Help me." He huffs.

"I'm tryin'. You need to go to the hospital."

He pulls his face close to mine. "No. No. Take me there." He points toward the trees.

CHAPTER FOUR

Void

This cannot be happening.

This cannot be happening.

God, this cannot be happening.

I pause for a moment to get some of my strength and energy back while still holding onto the guy. His arm around my shoulder is cramping my neck and there's an ache right behind my kneecap.

"I need a break." I huff and gently ease him on the ground in a pile of newly dropped pine needles that should feel like a cushion underneath his ass. I, exhausted, lean up against the strong leg of a hundred-year-old tree, close my eyes, and lightly breathe as I assess my situation. Being in the forest feels haunting especially having never gone into it-not even to camp-in all of my life. How could such a crowded place feel so isolated? Every crunch, thump, and snap from a distance and up close is heard like a sudden alarm that startles me. Who knows what else could be in here if *he* emerged from the forest like a mysterious relic.

I should leave him here. Take off without looking back since he's wounded and can't run after me, get in my car and stay indoors for months until he forgets my face. Yet the angel on my shoulder tells me to correct what I've caused.

There's an abrupt snap that yanks me out of my thoughts. Like someone stepped on a twig. I swiftly spin my head in several directions to see if anyone followed us into the forest, but realize the guy is doing something that requires him to lean over. As the snapping continue, I look to see him gripping his bent leg and winding it back into place. That's what's causing the sounds. He flexes his bent wrist, and it contorts straightforward, each finger moving as if they weren't broken close to impairment.

"JESUS CHRIST!"

"Shhhh." He puts a finger to his lip. He starts coughing and wheezing. Slowly he stands back up and I see that he's massive. There's no outrunning him. His calves and legs are muscular. Blood from a thick wound so deep bone is exposed through torn flesh and muscles, still rivers down the front of his face. The man's eyes roll back, he stumbles as if to faint and falls against a tree not too far from me. So, I can outrun him, but this damn angel on my shoulder. Whatever campsite he wants me to take him back to, it better surpass the basic standards of the county hospital.

I throw his arm over my shoulder, grateful he has working legs, and not all of his weight is on my weak body, but he smells like shit, and his breath is hot against my cheek. I wonder who the hell am I carrying? Superman?

He wheezes, "a little further" and we continue on.

The forest is nearly dark except for the sun shining through spaces between the pine leaves. Birds sing and the rapid flutter of them taking off from branches to midair catches my attention, away from the weird situation I've found myself in. I raise my eyes to see three birds all leaving from underneath the roof of greenery into the world above the trees. Down below, as I continue to carry the guy, I search for something brown in them mist of multi-toned bark. There're twigs snapping and I don't think I'm the only one causing the sound. Deer? Montana is filled with mountain lions. I've always wanted to go camping and hunting. Never imagined my first in depth forest exploration to be like this.

The cloth material of my shoes is soaked from stepping in puddles of mud, and my jacket gets caught on a loose branch, tearing the leather that's already tainted with this man's blood. His skull is still oozing, but he manages to keep conscious. His breathing is light as well as his steps, but I suppose with determination and willpower, they are keeping him from passing out.

I pray this man isn't taking me into a dangerous situation since I am helping him out in one of the oddest way possible. Maybe he's from a hidden commune that refuses to get with the current times. Cannibals perhaps? His shoes look handmade, his plaid pants, although tattered, must have come from somewhere outside of the forest unless he stole them from a camper before feasting on their flesh.

No.

I'm thinking too far into horror and scaring myself.

The sun has become completely invisible, and my surrounds are no longer a comfortable dim. I can't see anything past maybe three rows of trees before me and what lies up head is utter darkness as if a void wall stands in the distance. A black wall.

There's really a black wall a couple of feet in front of me that stretches for miles at each side.

"What the hell is that?" I say and push my foot back to stop.

It's unfamiliar and frightening, but the guy urges me to keep moving.

The muddy ground soon turns into a small stream that the man tells me to follow. I walk along the path, my heart slamming against my chest as the black wall gets closer and the air around us becomes thin. The sound of water moving underneath my feet serves as a little stress relief, but it's still coming up on me.

The guy's arm is draped tight around my shoulder and he's limping faster.

The black wall gets bigger. The magnificence of it makes me want to scream.

It's a void.

The unknown!

I take one final step to it and fall waist deep into a glittering clear pond.

I leap out and scurry back on my ass, gaping at the towering hedge of bush as high as a one-story building, stretching from the right and to the left as far as I could see, and shrinking into the horizon. Finally, some sunlight drops down on the area and shines a light on everything. I've hit a hedge wall and there's nothing but trees barely visible due to a heavy fog on the other side. It's like I hit a barrier or something.

The grass underneath me is livelier, almost like it's fake emerald green and spirals at the pointed ends. The pond at my ankles is glittering underneath, so clear I can see the land beneath the water. Strange spider-like bugs and centipedes float on the surface.

The bizarreness of it nearly makes me forget I'm with

company. The guy kneels down and bathes himself in the water. I watch and listen to him laugh in joy, wondering why he refused to go to the hospital to wash himself in a pond.

I glance at the glistening water and something shining between the rocks catches my attention. I lean towards the pond and dip my fingers into the lukewarm water to pick up the object. It's a transparent stone. When I take it out, my hand starts to tingle as if thousands of critters are walking along every crack and crevice of my skin around my fingers and palm. The markings of age completely vanish right before my eyes.

"What the hell?"

My skin is tight, and my fingers can flex without ache. I look down in the water for more translucent stones. There are dozens of them of all sizes.

"Stop." The guy says. His voice as deep as thunder. He is standing on both of his legs and the leakage from his head has stopped.

I take a step back, feeling my ankle being submerged in the pond. He takes one step closer to me with eyes that have averted from helplessness to hostile. I slowly place the rock in my pocket and meet his stance. He may be bigger than me, but I shouldn't be a threat to him considering I helped his ass back to this healing spot. Now, I need answers.

"Who are you?" I question.

He doesn't answer with eyes bolted on me, eyebrows low and fist clenched.

I raise my hands and nervously chuckle. I ask something different. Anything to keep him calm. "Look, I'm sorry for what happened. I should've been paying attention."

He remains mute, but even his silence is threatening.

"What is that water?"

He still doesn't say anything. Instead, he raises his right hand and points his finger in the direction that we came from. He wants me to leave. Why? I glance back at the pond and see more shining rocks. I can't leave now, not after discovering what could be a diamond mine and possibly the fountain of youth if this fucker was healed just from splashing in it.

I raise a finger. "Hold on."

I turn around and start walking deeper into the pond. My legs, the aches in my ankles and the rock in the back of my kneecaps instantly fade the further the water rises up my jeans. I can't leave. I gotta get at least two more rocks to take and get inspected. If I came onto something, I could finally help my mother, move out, and become that rich bachelor with a bunch of chicks begging to lay beside me.

A fierce growl sends a jolt to my heart and before I can get a chance to look back, the guy lunges himself at me!

I don't have the time to jump out of the way. He grabs my jacket, yanks me out of the pond, and wraps his arm around my neck. His forearm pushes against my throat and he tightens his muscles to cut off my airway. With all of his weight on my body, but for once in my life, even after years of not working out, my legs are stronger than they have ever been, and I keep myself on my feet.

"What..." I gasp. "What the hell are...

He tightens the chokehold and starts speaking a language I don't understand.

I fight with every bit of strength I have, but my body is weakening. It hurts. My chest is cramping, and I feel my heart thumping erratically. I open my eyes. My vision is blackening, and, at that moment, time shifts my thoughts from curiosity to terror. My sullen face to my mother's toothless smile.

This man is going to kill me.

This is what being choked to death feels like.

An endless struggle between an inflamed body that is being consumed with intensity from panic and the weight of someone's wrath against me. All while this is happening, I hear the guy who I saved. He is still speaking the strange language like a lullaby to the afterlife.

I close my eyes and allow my body to go limp. He releases his grasp and drops me to the ground. A bug wandering in the moist earth crawls over the tips of my fingers, so I know I'm not dead, but I keep my eyes closed. Fallen leaves rustle with movement all around me and I still hear the voice of the guy, but I sense his presence fade just a bit before I open my eyes again. He is at the pond with his hands in the water. I take in a large breath of air to get my strength back and slowly grab onto a heavy stone.

So much for having a clean conscious.

I slam the rock against the fucker's head and watch him go down. The blow was hard enough to knock him to his side, but he is still conscious, now jolted with confusion.

I stand over him and shout, "I helped you man!"

For what it's worth, the fucker deserves to die.

I slam the rock against his skull repeatedly, feeling warm liquid fly onto my cheeks, and continue until his face is no longer recognizable to anyone who could have known him.

The pond. If it was able to heal him once, I'm making sure it doesn't heal him again. I throw the rock back, drag him into a cluster of bushes, and wipe his blood and dirt off on my jeans.

"Should have let me take the fucking rocks." I mumble and

kick him over and over again with the heal of my shoe using every piece of strength I have in my legs. For my mother, my father, my crappy life.

Emotionally relieved, I step back into the pond to wash my hands off.

The water is so warm and easing to my stirred mind. I cup my hands, collect more water, and douse my face feeling instantly fresh. A light breeze blows, drying the water and standing still, it's as if a thousand bugs are running all over my face, gripping the loose skin at the corners and underneath my eyes, the crown of my head and under my chin to pull it all back behind my ears. I don't feel tired anymore. Who knew hanging skin would make someone feel older.

For the first time in twenty years, I'm awake and touching the smoothness of my face brings a sense of liveliness back to me. What if I did stumble upon something like the fountain of youth? Despite the filthy surroundings of the forest, the water is as clear as a mountain top spring. If the guy was willing to kill to keep me from it, then something is special about the water and the stones at the bottom.

For a moment, I gaze at my hands and flex my fingers. Wind blows and cools my damp skin, I see more markings like liver spots and accidental scars vanish. I flex my fingers again and feel no cramping of my joints. I gasp and whisper, "wow." I have to come back with a bottle. This water *is* special and the most important person who could use it is Carol for her joints, but for now while I'm here, my mind shifts into collecting more rocks.

I walk further into the pond and pick up as many stones that I can find. I'm waist deep in the water, but I don't mind. It feels so good and heals my body, especially at my hips and tailbone. My pockets become heavy from the weight of the rocks, but my legs are strong that they feel as light as feathers, and I see one larger than all the others I have collected. My eyes widen with a mixture of shock and happiness. That one could be it. The one that grants me millions if they are real diamonds. But I have to dive completely underwater to get it.

After inspecting the area and concluding that it's just me and the wildlife, I inhale and dive underwater.

The pond is deeper than I expected, but clear enough for me to see the rock sitting at the bottom, dazzling at me while being surrounded by nothing but earth from the neck up. I kick and kick as my body becomes lighter and tighter. Each lounge forward pushes me closer and faster to my goal. Not only have I strengthened, my stamina is as if I'm a kid again running a mile and back without stopping. I wrap my fingers around the stone and give it one tug, but it doesn't budge, not even with two hands and after I've dug my fingers into the earth around it.

I pull it harder, but it seems to be glued to the bottom. I need air, so I raise my body up, but my back presses against something. The man? Frightened, I turn around and see the surface of the pond. Outside no one is there. I raise my hand to free it from the water, however my palm presses against the clear sheet.

What the fuck! I can't get out of the water.

I think I'm under a sheet of ice or something. I continue to push both of my hands against the film but it's solid.

God, as much as I want to freak out, I can't, or I am going to drown. Holding my breath for dear life, I look underwater for another opening. The pond continues on further, so I start swimming, but I have to reach for the large rock one more time. I pull at it again, but it doesn't move. Damn. If I die, I at least want my corpse to turn up with something other than the waterlogged remains of a loser. I can already feel myself running out of oxygen.

I push my arms and kick my feet harder. The water darkens the further I get, but I see a light at the end of the way. Please let it be a way out because I feel my lungs back in the moment I was being choked to death.

Oh God, please don't let me face oncoming death again.

Give me air. My chest is on fire and the only thing I can do is open my mouth. Water fills my lungs and sets them ablaze.

Sorry I didn't come back with your package, Carol.

I shut my eyes and take on death peacefully.

CHAPTER FIVE

Monster

We're all given at least three chances to make something out of ourselves in this life. I've only seen the first and let it slip from my fingers. It's not fair.

My mother reaches out to me. I lay in bed looking at her but not feeling right about my bedroom. The walls are foggy.

****

A bubble crawls up my esophagus and when I belch, water splashes all over my face. I can breathe. I take in gulps of air while thanking God for letting me live. Or am I dead? Laying on my back, I open my eyes, but they're burned by a bright light above me. The natural flare from the sun rays blurs my vision. I can feel pain, so I'm alive.

I open my eyes wider and look around with my hand raised over my eyebrows for shade. There are more trees above and around me. Shit, I'm still in the forest, and it's hauntingly darker except for the tiny glimpses of the world seeing through the sun's rays. My right palm brushes against damp grass and I breathe in some of the freshest air my lungs have ever tasted. I think my unconscious body floated to the end of the pond or maybe I'm on the other side of the hedge, yet I honestly still don't know if I'm dead or alive. There's an inviting sound of soft whooshing and splattering near me. Not too far from me is an isolated stream of water falling from the sky, through the tops of the trees, and hitting the surface of the pond. Is this what heaven looks like? The place where your last breath was taken. But I don't understand. I can't see past the trees that encircle me. I can't see what's coming or watching me, yet I feel like I'm being observed.

Crack!

I turn around and gasp. A pair of massive black circles is before my face. A presence stronger than an icy blast of oncoming wind in the middle of winter hits me and suddenly I can't breathe as I fall into an abyss of sparkling darkness. The face of a monster. Brown skinned, tiny nose and large lips. Four branches like antlers protrude out the sides of its head.

It raises its hand as I struggle to move my tense body. The only control I have is my fingers that I dig into the moist earth. I can't turn away. It's worse than looking at the fucking wall. Hypnotically unfamiliar as if I'm looking at a decaying corpse of a stranger. I'm in hell and the only thing I can do is stand still as the monster moves its hand closer to my agape mouth. A berry wrapped in a bright green leaf between its fingers.

My jaw drops to let out a scream of terror and the monster swiftly shoves the fruit down my throat, and I feel my tight muscles loosen in a matter of seconds.

My arms can't hold my body.

I'm sinking.

My head rests on something firm and warm.

And my eyes close again.

The best thing I ever ate was my mother's spaghetti and meatballs when I was eleven years old. I had just come in from school. It was raining and cold outside. My father was in the den-this was before he was sent off to war, reading the newspaper. He didn't say anything to me. Probably didn't care that I was soaking wet, near sick, and heartbroken he didn't pick me up from school. I walked past him, following the scent of garlic and green onions straight into the kitchen where I found my mother was standing at the stove. She didn't hear me come in. The compelling symphonies of Mozart were flowing into her ears from the radio. As she hummed and swished her hips from side to side, I pulled on her floral apron to get her attention.

She saw my condition, was overcome with sympathy, and dropped everything in her hands.

"Aw my baby." Carol knelt down to be eye-level with me. She placed her warm hand gently on my soaked cold cheek. "I'm sorry. From now on, I'll pick you up." My mother whispered into my ear.

She directed me to go to my room and get into a pair of warm clothes. I did as commanded, came back into the kitchen and on the table, there was a plate of spaghetti and meatballs made for me. The steam rising from the dish was like a finger enticing me to come over and consume. The first bite into a hunk of warm meat felt like Heaven. A place where all of my worries and past misery faded into a void. I came in feeling hatred for my father, but at that moment, sitting with my mother and eating her delicious food shifted my attitude from fury to relaxation. It felt like my hardened soul was turning to ooze. I looked at my mother. She mouthed the words "I love you with all of my heart".

My head is inclined and under my skull there is firmness. Better than my ten-year-old pillow against my neck. I keep my eyes closed feeling a sense of relaxation that I once felt as a child resting on a summery afternoon.

What the hell just happened?

Shit. There's trees, but at least my body doesn't feel like it turned into stone. Although I'm too relaxed to move, I accept it. I can't think straight. I think I had a bad dream. But…I'm still in the forest. Just close my eyes and I'll probably wake up in my bed. As long as I don't see anything, none of this matters.

I'm not in pain anymore.

The air is crisp mixed with the scent of sycamore, dew and cucumbers and I'm reminded of a time when my mother attempted to make a salad for Roger. It was full of luscious green with dabs of red from the grape tomatoes for contrast. He yelled at her, saying he wasn't a rabbit, and I ate the dish instead feeling lost energy instantly restored once I flushed everything down with a cup of water and I was back outside with my friends feeling livelier than ever. Thats how I feel now. Refreshed. I move my ankles and feel the lightness of them and water between my toes. My legs are back in the pond. Fuck. How many times will I black out until I awaken no more?

A smile grows across my face at the memory, and my body suddenly shudders under the tickle of someone's touch. One hand is on the crown of my head and the other lightly grazes the side of my face, down my cheek, along my neck-stopping at my Adam's Apple-before resting over my thumping heart.

I sigh, taking in all of their warmth radiating from their fingers and slowly open my eyes to see a pair of nicely seated breasts over my face.

"It's awake." A low voice echoes in my head and once again, fear strikes me, but I can't look away from the body I'm resting on. A woman. She looked over her chest down at me.

"Where is the man?" She questions.

I slowly rise up from her thighs and look hard into her brown face. "W-who the are you?"

She doesn't say anything.

I must be dead in my version of heaven because there is no one else who walks the earth that matches her beauty. Doe eyes that brighten like embers in the light, wide lips with perfect symmetrical puffiness, and skin like melting dark chocolate. As she moves her face closer to mine, her wild bush of hair brushes up against my forehead. I hear her light breathing and take in her scent of nature.

I lean back and slowly raise my hand with caution combined with fascination. This could be an angel I'm about to touch. She raises an eyebrow as I draw my hand closer to her face. My eyes shift to her breast. They are so perky. I have to touch them. I mean, she's sitting here naked except for a sheer piece of fabric that drapes over her body. I had my head resting inches from her private area. Whether this is a dream or I'm in heaven, I have to meet my skin with hers to confirm the better-I'm dead and God has accepted me to live amongst his angels. Or this could be a cheap trick from the devil in disguise.

"Do not touch her." The low voice says again.

My eyes lock onto something furry and white behind her.

A short yelp, I draw my hand back and scurry backwards until I'm reaching the edge where earth meets the pond.

A massive wolf is behind her! The size of a brown bear

and baring its sharp fangs.

Terrified, I point with a rattling finger as my gawk shifts from the pair of eyes on its face to the ones on its forehead.

The beast walks and sits beside the woman and again I hear the low voice say, "You have doomed us all."

"Oh my, God." I bury my face between my legs, crouched and cowering within myself like an opossum. Maybe if I don't move, it will not attack me. Just play dead. Maybe if I constantly tell myself to wake up, I will. Yet nothing happens. The thin air never turns thick with moisture from heavy rainfall and the pattering from the mysterious waterfall into the pond continues.

The woman snatches me by the hair and raises my head up.

"Where is the man?" The woman questions.

She gawks at me. The wolf is now calm, licking its paw and sneezes.

"Evil has found its way in." The voice comes from the animal as it turns its head to the woman and wheezes.

"A-am I dead." I ask.

Nothing like this happens in reality. I know I'm not dreaming because I feel everything. The vibration of the water hitting the pond and the cool mist of it against my face. The warmth of the sun. The scent of fresh pine trees and new dirt that makes me think of my childhood days of digging in the ground for roly-polies fills my nostrils. The woman, how she looked at a rusted fellow like me, yet I felt her having compassion over me. Nothing like this exists in Montana. A grey world that smells like sulfur and festering lumber, at least in Greenwood.

The wolf looks at me. "You might as well be."

My jaw drops, my lungs tighten, and all I can do is sit

there with my mouth agape, wanting to scream at the top of my lungs, but nothing comes out. I gaze around as the world grows eerily vivid. The trees. God, the trees. I lift my eyes to the sky and stare at the frozen explosions of green bubbles overhead. Sunlight slices through the leaves like fiery lasers, glimmering and pulsing like veins.

I close my mouth and inhale deeply. The air is so fresh, laced with the crisp mist of the waterfall. There's a wolf speaking human words, yet somehow the forest has stripped away any instinct to feel afraid. I should be screaming my fucking lungs out. Instead, all I want is to sink into the atmosphere, to breathe in and out as the trees do around me, with the wolf and maybe its mother earth standing close by.

Birdsong weaves through the air. Twigs snap under the weight of curious wildlife. Eight swans bathe in the pond, each sweep of their wings sending ripples that melt my mind into a state of contentment and being. Moments ago, I was exhausted and caged. Now, all I want is to skip through the rows of greenery and dance beneath the cool pond water.

I open my eyes wider and feel the warmth of liquid beads roll down my cheeks.

"I feel…free." I whisper and turn away to clean my face. I don't want this woman to see me cry. I have to pull it together. Roger would've cursed me if I were to cry in front of him. Crying is a form of weakness in his eyes and I can't let him or anyone see me weep, but it's hard to contain this anguish when it's been festering in my soul for so many years.

The woman places her hand on my shoulders. "Where is the man?" She says again. Her voice is like an angel strumming a harp.

I keep my head lowered. God, what have I done?

"Leave him be." I hear the beast say. "You have opened his eye and now he has to come to terms with his existence."

I move my gaze around the waterfall, searching for where it's coming from, but all that's there nestled above the trees is a single cloud. What wonder did I come into or am I dead? My mind can't wrap around what's happening and the things that's around me. All I know is I'm eerily calm to four eyed animals, a monster with large eyes wandering around in the woods-or maybe it was the woman- and a waterfall coming from a floating cloud.

My eyes then fall into a thick branch hanging over the pond and wrapped around its arm are two nooses that gently rock back and forth in the wind.

I gasp and avert my gaze back to the woman and her beast.

"Go. There is more work to be done before nightfall." The wolf slowly steps up to me. I lean back with my hand raised slightly before my chest.

The woman nods, grabs the handle of her basket full of leaves, berries, and fruits grown from trees. Mangoes and apples. I hardly ever see them and not as freshly skinned as the ones she possesses. She rises from her crouched position, becoming as tall and thick with long legs I want to graze with my pinky finger. She walks off giving me one last worried glance and trots down a row spacing of more greenery.

The wolf sits beside me and looks outward into the forest before us. As more light is cast through the trees, the better I can see that it isn't an ordinary garden.

The pond continues its stream outward and branches off like a circulatory system of the human body, spreading to different locations throughout the land. There are bushes housing berries of all kinds, ripe and dripping from collected haze. The woman carefully walks up and down the dirt paths. She digs in her basket and throws small pellets onto the ground. She's gardening. As she leaves the treated row, little stems of green instantly sprout from the ground. Maybe she's tossing fertilizer, but something strange.

The plants, leaves, branches, stems twirl when the glittering substances she throws land on them as if they are responding with gratitude.

Everything is alive here and twice the size of normalcy.

"Where am I?"

The wolf runs his long tongue against its fangs. "A fragment of new beginnings." It turns its head to me. "Trusted in her hands. Where is her helper? Without him, the garden will be consumed and cease to exist. Life in need of it will surely die."

I shake my head. "I don't know what you're talking about?"

The wolf growls. "Liar!"

I quickly move a couple of paces away from the animal with my hands up for protection.

"I smell his scent on your hands. You cannot fool one which has been appointed to aid and protect the husbandman and his helper. I sense all, I know all. Your body is filthy. You do not belong the garden."

"Yulisi!"

I look over my shoulder. The woman rejoins us without her basket, but in its loss a swan walks as elegantly as her close by.

"Send him back." The bird says through a soft female voice. "I will see he makes it to the other side." It dives and disappears underwater.

The wolf snarls.

"Man?" She says to her pet.

The wolf turns to her. "We are sending him back to find him."

There's a snap of a twig somewhere out in the distance that alarms the beast. He searches with his ears raised high in the air and tail stiff.

"Get him out of here!" The wolf takes off.

I look at the woman. She stares back at me with eyes full of sympathy. I don't want to leave her here alone. My eyes fall to her chest. Her breast looks so inviting.

She takes a couple of steps closer to me. Wedged between her thumb and index finger, the woman extends another leaf towards me without coming too close. I'm hesitant as well. The dog told me not to touch her, but I have to. She couldn't have been the monster I saw not too long ago.

The wolf returns and is standing close at her side. Its lips are twitching as a soft growl escapes through its clenched sharp teeth.

"Thank you." I gently slide my fingers down her smooth arm to her wrist, fingers, and take the leaf. She smiles and displays two rows of white teeth that shine like the diamonds in the pond and lowers her arms to her side. I step forward. "Please." I say and reach to touch her cheek. "Tell me what's your-

"Enough." The wolf snarls and starts to trudge towards me. "Bring the man back. Do not return without him."

Looking at the beast quiver as it growls, I realize he has been communicating with me through my mind. No wonder why I can hear his voice so fucking clear as if it's my own conscious.

I stuff the leaf into my jacket's pocket and take backward

steps. I keep my eyes focused on the wolf's yellow iris like looking at the sun through a high-powered telescope and seeing parts of the molten rock explode. The second set of its eyes are murky white.

One last step backwards and my heel sinks into the earth. I lose my balance, arms swing wildly in the air as if reaching from something invisible to grab onto, and I fall into the pond.

Naturally, I would float to the surface, but that film is back over it, hard as ice making it impossible to pierce my body through just like before on the other side. However, I can still see through it. The woman leans over. Peering down, she smiles until the wolf beckons her to walk away with a long howl.

I feel like I can break the barrier given the water is restoring many years of lost strength.

Part of me wants to punch the glass until it shatters. It's solid like a sheet of ice over a frozen lake. Underwater, in the fountain of youth, I feel powerful enough to and everything breaks under pressure. But my swings with the push back of water will do no damage.

I was in a beautiful place with a woman who seemed to be so innocent and helpless. Rarely do I find something like her in my world. Why the hell would I, or anyone for that matter, want to go back to reality? Reality is where the sun is covered with a dusky grey cloud throughout majority of the year. Anytime the sun did shine, it's only temporary until it rained again and the showers don't smell crisp. Rainfall felt heavy on the body as if the toxins from manufacture plants replaced the purity of the atmosphere.

I follow the swan as far as it goes before the animal stops, taps its beak through the surface and waits for me to reach my hand up over the water. I wonder what would happen if I follow it back to the garden and stand up to the wolf. I am human after all with rejuvenated strength and man is supposed to be dominate over beast. But, what the hell kind of foolishness am I thinking?

I grasp onto the muddy ground and pull myself out of the pond, feeling sticky. My wet clothes cling tight onto my body, yet I feel what I've longed for since reaching thirty. Youthful. Most likely due to being completely submerged in the rejuvenating water.

I sit down on a fallen tree and take deep breaths in and out. I'm not exhausted. Trust me. Just basking in the ease of how oxygen flows through my lungs. I don't have a raspy cough like I use to. My arms and legs aren't tired from swishing and kicking through the water. I should take a swim in a bigger pond since I'm feeling like I'm twenty-one years old again, but all I do is remain seated on the tree trying to piece together what the fuck just happened.

On the other side, in reality, it's drizzling. I guess the forecast was right after all. Thick raindrops slip through nature's roofing and splatter down on all that's motionless around me. The pond, each drop forming a circular ripple. My already soaked jacket and head. That asshole who nearly killed me, still dead.

I stand up and step over him. The critters of the earth are already feasting on his flesh. A line of ants crawls out of his agape mouth while some are burrowing into the open wound inches above his temple where I bashed the rock.

"Shit." I whisper as it all comes back to me.

I killed someone.

CHAPTER SIX

Leaves

My car's been moved to the side of the road, turned off and has a yellow paper wedged between the windshield and wiper.

Seeing it from afar, I curse as I come out of the forest, tear a piece of already sliced leather from my black jacket, and tie it around a tree. How long was I gone and shit, how could I leave my car out in the middle of the road still running?

Oh yeah.

I sprint up to my vehicle, elated no punk drove off with it. There's a black bag inches from my back, drivers tire, and a small puddle of rain mixed with the blood of the guy still bright in color. It's all coming back to me now. The recollection of my car slamming forward sends shivers down my spine.

I hit someone.

"Shit." I scoop up the bag that's actually a woven basket made of twigs, fused together with a black substance, like tar. Inside there are more leaves like the one the woman gave me. My eyes grow wide and there's a tickle in my nostrils from the sweet aroma I don't recall smelling before. These types of leaves are different, covered in tiny black beads and curl inward at the tips.

I assume these plants have ripened past the correct amount of time unlike the one I was given, yet I'm sure they are still good to consume. If anything, the potency of the plant might have increased for the better with their age.

I close the lid, toss the basket in the back of my trunk and drive off to Jerry's house. Carol must be having a conniption. It never takes me more than an hour to and from Jerry's spot. The yellow paper is a ticket for fifty dollars I don't have.

*****

I knock three times on the red painted door and cough. Hearing thumping and clanging on the other side, Katrina opens the door wearing nothing but a large black t-shirt that has BANG over her chest and mismatched socks. Her blonde wavy hair drapes over her shoulders and her brown eyes widen as she looks me up and down as if I crawled out of a grave. I *was* close to a watery grave and I'm still wearing some of the mud on my yellow shirt that's dried up.

"Are you alright?" She asks.

"Yeah." I say. "Where's Jerry?"

Katrina's eyes travel from my face down to my shoes and I see her bottom lip shift side to side.

"Hold on." She slams the front door on my face.

I hear more thumping and faint voices on the other side.

Nervous, I tap my hand rapidly against the side of my leg and look around at the area.

This is the ghettos of Greenwood. If I go further down that one-way street in the opposite direction from my own home, it gets just as worse. Roads filled with potholes, weatherbeaten houses littered with either the homeless or hookers. After that is the highway, straight to the city.

There's already a crowd hovering in the parking lot, probably close friends with Jerry. I keep my eyes forward and aside from feeling uncomfortable in this area, I'm starting to feel like shit. I ran over someone. They're probably examining my appearance the way Katrina just did. Maybe they know, can see it on me.

A man is dead because of me.

That thought refuses to leave my mind. I left his corpse at the foot of his door. His face under my boot flashes before my eyes and suddenly my stomach is churching. I haven't had a full decent meal since last night, if I can count fast food from a tired-out restaurant decent.

The processed food, plus the orange juice from this morning, and possibly the natural chemicals from the raw plant and garden-fresh fruit all combined together are like a battle taking place in the pits of my bowels. Sharp twinges jab in my stomach as it digests the food. The ache then travels down my intestines like a bolder rolling down a cliff.

I lean against the door frame with one hand and the other, my arm wrapped around my waist. I only close my eyes for a second, and when I reopen them, my vision is back to its blurred state. God, it feels like my body is back to what it once was, but doubled the weight, exhaustion, and inner emotional turmoil. Everything is so fucking messed up and I can really use a nap.

Jerry yanks open the door, nearly ripping it off its rusted hinges.

"Uh, are you alright?" He asks, gaping down at me.

I suck it up and stand straight. I'm five foot six and two-forty in giggly mass. Jerry, on the other-hand towers over me by six more inches and one fifty pounds of balanced muscle and fat. I remember him telling me that he was a football player in high school. That's how he got bulky. The chicks use to dig him like how they adored me and my band mates, but due to unfortunate life changing circumstances, shit happened.

My band mates and all of our hopes and dreams of becoming successful broke when one had a snot-nosed brat and wanted to start a family. Jerry's dream of playing in the league ended when he broke his right leg. The depression of being off the field hindered his recovery and now he walks with a limp. He's a loser like me. Living in a weather-beaten apartment on the shitty side of town selling loose cigarettes and weed. The only difference between him and I other than being thirteen years apart is his access to cooch every night under his own roof. But for me, that's all about to change. This makes me smile. However, I don't know if they will believe me.

Like his girlfriend, Jerry wears a black shirt with the words BANG printed in large white letters and black jogging pants stained with white blotches of paint. He demands to know where the hell I was for the last couple of hours. Carol has been calling non-stop on my whereabouts not out of concern for my wellbeing, but her packages eta. It's going on two in the afternoon; the usual time she would make a large lunch for Roger and throw his ass in the bed for a nap like a four-year-old child. In his medicated induced slumbers, Carol would put on headphones and clean the house while listening to symphonies she used to dance to. I have to remind her to do my laundry today.

Katrina points her tiny finger at me. She has her nails painted black. "Baby. Look at his eyes." She tells Jerry.

He raises an eyebrow and narrows his. I look back and

forth between them.

"What's wrong with my eyes?"

"Are you doing that heavy shit?" Jerry questions. He raises his chest as if that's supposed to frighten me. Katrina moves behind him and grabs onto his tattoo covered arm.

"No. I'm dirty as hell and my stomach hurts." I snap. Aw man, it's like someone dumped two more rocks into my stomach. They're floating in the acid and bouncing off the walls of my guts. "I need to use your bathroom."

Jerry moves to the side and Katrina shouts for me to take off my shoes.

I beeline straight to the bathroom and plop my ass down on the toilet.

Like the entire house, the bathroom is a mess. The lower half of the mirror is covered in white stains; I assume from toothpaste. The porcelain sink has black blotches from Katrina's hair die before she went blonde. The counter is lined with hair products and mechanics like a flat iron, curlers, hair clippers, a can of Comet cleaner, and brushes.

Rarely do I ever use their bathroom-even step into their house. It's never clean, smells like burned cookies, or their cat Biscuit is wandering around making those weird howling noises that pisses me off for some reason. I'm not fond of cats.

I always make the exchange at the door. My stomach has forced me to step into their boarders and although it's hurting like hell, nothing is coming out despite the pressure I feel against my asshole. This is something I have to let work itself through.

I wash my hands and look at myself in the mirror. Particularly my eyes which caused the couple to freak out. I stand there stunned myself. The blue of my irises has been reduced to a thin circular line. My pupils have expanded wide as if I had injected a harder drug like ecstasy. Could it have been from the plant I ate in the forest? Was I on a strong natural drug that made me hallucinate the entire ordeal?

Fuck. I don't know.

That can't be the case. I've taken ecstasy one time in my younger years while I was at a concert with the boys. The drug made me want to touch everything and dance until I didn't have the energy to no longer stand. Everything was illuminated. The lights from the stage, the music from the drums and guitars, the singer's voice that vibrated through the environment.

When I was in the forest, everything was euphoric, but uncontrollable and frightening, staring back at me past my exterior and into my soul to judge me. I didn't hear animals talk on ecstasy.

I remove my shirt and wash my face. As I'm walking out of the bathroom, Katrina is holding a pair of tattered jogging pants and a worn-out shirt. She is hesitant on handing the clothes over to me.

"You…didn't kill anyone did you?" She asks. I shake my head no. "Then why are you wet?"

I snatch the clothes from her. "Stop asking stupid questions." I say and slam the bathroom door in her face.

Back to my reflection, I run my fingers along the smoothness of my face. Under my eyes, it's no longer puffy. I have a head full of curly brown hair and as I run my fingers through the softness, I shiver at a recollection of my first lover. She sat on my lap facing me. I rested my head on her chest and melted in her embrace.

"Who did you get this beautiful hair from?" she asked.

I didn't answer. She didn't need to know it was from my mother. At the time, after a long performance, all I wanted from her was her warm body.

I quickly change my clothes. In my pants pocket, I remove the leaf now crumpled and hand it to Katrina. Jerry is in the bedroom doing something with the door cracked and we are in the kitchen. The smell of cooking weed in the oven burns the thin hairs of my nose. After a while of sitting in this house, one can become high themselves just from breathing in the fumes.

"Take a look at this." I say.

Katrina looks down at the plant and twirls it by the stem between her fingers. "What's this?"

I lean on the kitchen counter and wipe a couple of breadcrumbs onto the floor. "I don't know. I was hoping you would be the one to tell me that."

"It's a leaf."

"No shit, sherlock. Can you tell me what type of leaf it is?"

"Do I look like a wildlife expert?"

I sigh, move closer to Katrina, and say in a low tone of voice. "It's the reason why I look like this."

I have to tell her what happened. Even if I look like a crazy buffoon. But Katrina is the type of person who is on the eccentric side. I know she believes in crazy outer-worldly shit like multiple dimensions, astrology, and crystals.

She gives me her full attention while I tell her the entire story. I do alter how it started saying I ran over a deer and felt so bad, I dragged it back into the forest by its antlers. She scoffs and raises a single eyebrow. It's completely out of my character to feel bad for animals. I ran over a squirrel who darted out in the street and kept going with a grin on my face. I glower at the sight of her cat who seems to always be in heat whenever I come around. Dogs are just as worse.

Once I finish my story and look her dead in the eyes for a

reaction, the realization settles in on me that I must've passed out sometime between being in the water or getting strangled and lost some braincells, yet how could that be possible? Everything did happen, even up to this moment standing before her twirling the leaf in her hand. That should be confirmation that a strange place like that exists.

Katrina only smirks and raises the leaf up one more time over her head to get a good look at it under the bright kitchen light.

"Must be some good shit if you saw all that." I hear Jerry behind me and spin around. He walks into the kitchen, and my eyes fall onto a black gun in his right hand. "Talking animals, a garden in this shit town. A woman, *naked* coming close to your ass. Yeah right. You sure you didn't take some strong shit before coming here, crashed in a ditch and dream all that up?"

"If you don't believe me," I nod my head towards the plant. "Eat it."

Katrina raises the plant up to her lips. Jerry, with wide eyes, takes a step closer. "Don't eat that."

"Wrap it up in some food." I say. "I don't know how it tastes on its own."

I hear a click and there's a cold barrel shoved against my temple. I freeze and raise my hands. Jerry grabs a handful of the shirt's collar and holds it tight. He presses the gun harder against my head and yanks at me so close to his face, I can feel his breath on my ear.

"If anything happens to her, I'll blow what little brains you have left all over this floor, fat ass."

He nods his head at his girl, giving her the ok the eat the plant.

She looks highly nervous.

Uncertain, Katrina opens her mouth and nearly shoves it through her teeth until I shout that she has to eat it with something just as I did. Maybe a piece of fruit or chewy candy. She opens the refrigerator and pulls out a brownish-red strawberry with wilting leaves. I would have opted to eat it with a piece of candy rather than an old fruit and I honestly don't know how it will affect the plant in general. The woman in the forest gave me a fresh-looking seedless plum that dominated the overall sensation of one eating a raw leaf and its taste.

As Katrina chews on both substances, her eyes narrow and her closed mouth twist in an expression of disgust, but I see her throat rise for a moment and drop down.

"Wouldn't it be logical to have 911 dialed up if something-

Jerry yanks at my collar now choking me. "What the hell for, man? You said it wouldn't hurt her."

I still have my hands raised feeling my heart racing and intestine churning the little food I had. I shrug my shoulders and chuckle. "Just saying."

Trying to keep this calm composure while wanting to shit all over myself is like juggling on a ball. My ass cheeks are squeezed tight and it's like my feet have fused to the ground while Jerry is rocking slightly. Up close, his breath smells like beer as a gust of it rolls over my shoulder. This fucker might twitch while his finger is on the trigger.

"Jerry," Katrina finally says in her soft tone of voice. She pours herself a cup of water and guzzles it down. "I'm fine. Put the gun away."

"You sure?"

She nods her head.

Jerry removes the gun, but I still sense its cold barrel pressed against my temple and an oncoming throbbing headache. We then stare at the young woman for any signs of delirium. She doesn't find anything disturbing about our raised eyebrows and deep gazes of speculation towards her calm demeanor. I think back to my first reaction to the plant. I cried like a mid-twenty-year-old realizing the true hardships of adulthood. How truly fucked up my life is in the glory of the world, the garden and all of its magnificence. We are in a different setting though and only two pairs of eyes are looking back at her versus hundreds.

Will Katrina see the world as I did through what seemed like wide open eyes with the film of distortion created by society removed. I felt pitiful. Less than a man and more like a child sitting beside the mother of nature.

Thank God the doorbell rings.

Jerry walks out of the kitchen leaving me alone with his girlfriend. She is gawking at me. Her brown eyes begin to glimmer, and the corner of her bottom lip starts to twitch. I take a step back closer to the kitchen door. If this girl has a negative reaction towards the drug, I can haul ass towards the exit while Jerry has his guard down.

As he's in his room most likely weighing out a bag, I glance down the hall to see the front door open. There stands one of Jerry's regular customers I once ran past on my way to my car a couple of weeks ago. She's a young fair skinned, brown haired woman that is a little on the chunky side. I remember her so well because of a large off colored rose she had tattooed on her neck that looked like a strange birthmark from afar.

I turn my gaze back to Katrina. She is leaning against the kitchen sink with her arms folded across her chest. Her head is lowered but shining trails stretch from her eyes to her chin.

"Everything alright?" I ask.

She raises her head showing me her bloodshot eyes, nods her head, and sweeps the back of her hands across her face. It smears tears and a thin line of snot across her face.

"Did this happen to you too?" she asks with a sniff.

I lower my eyes. "Yeah."

"What is this feeling?"

I shrug and look deeply at Katrina. I don't know if I'm still feeling the effects from the plant (I ate it nearly three hours ago) but Katrina isn't a bad looking girl. Why haven't I seen her this way, even though I've been here a number of times for my mother? I have no clue, but the reason behind that could be due to the fact that I never *really* examined her. If I did stare too long, Jerry's gun would be up against my face, threatening to gouge out my eyes for looking at his girl like a mere object.

Katrina is someone I wouldn't mind having at my side. In contrast with her guy, she's a kindhearted, young woman with an aura of innocence, probably due to her height under five feet and petite frame. I can understand why Jerry is with her. If he's anything like me, he's battling an internal war with the weight being a failure in life. Lost, and hopeless for anything better for ourselves.

One could cuddle against her and confess their deepest secrets without feeling a sense of judgment or pity, but acceptance. I always liked how her brown eyes brought out the fairness of her skin. As she's crying now, those blood shot scalars and the film of tears only makes those eyes glimmer like a cluster of stars.

"How does it feel?" I ask.

She shrugs and pushes out a soft laughter through the need to break down and cry a little more. "Kind of good. I was about to start my period and was feeling kind of like blah. Where did you get the plant from again?"

"In the forest. You know. The back roads."

"Strange. Why would it be *here* of all places."

Yeah, I know. That garden looked as if its's never known a single season. Here we are in the middle of spring, soggy grounds and weather like a bipolar teen on the west side of Montana. At first, I thought it was heaven, but it could have been mistaken for someone's backyard in Honolulu, Hawaii.

"I feel like...everything is going to be alright with myself." Katrina continues on. "I don't have anymore pains. I can't think of anything wrong that I can't change or even want to change myself. I'd rather let whatever is happening solve itself out without me being involved. Do you have anymore of that plant?"

I shake my head.

"Can you get more?"

Oh yeah! I snap my fingers. "I have a basket in my car. Hold on."

I run out of the apartment and retrieve the woven basket from my trunk. The smell of the plants are strong, but sweet, like sniffing a fresh basil plant.

I carry it back into the apartment, set it down on the kitchen table, and open the top for Katrina to look down into.

She pulls out one spiral plant coated in little black beads and narrows her eyes. The plants from the baskets are different than the one I had given her from my pants pocket. Katrina tells me it looks aged, but if it had the same effects as her lovely friend Mary Jane, then the potency should be stronger, just like I suspected. The plants aren't aging like fallen leaves from regular tree branches, but they are darker.

"I wonder what would happen if we smoked this?"

Katrina says. She is pulling off the tiny black beads that are about the same size as a mustard seed from each leaf and dumps them into a small ceramic bowl that looked to be made from a beginner taking a pottery class. I stand beside her and assist.

"I don't know, but I wouldn't try it." I shrug. "The effects might be different."

"Gene." Katrina says my name softly. I look down at her and see her pupils have expanded. She smiles and holds up a plant before my face. "You'll never know unless you try it. What if you found a new type of drug that isn't harmful at all, like a new type of cannabis plant. You know shit like that is growing in the rainforest. Natural vegetation that is keeping native tribes alive. Even they have their own mind-altering substances provided by earth."

"I doubt it. And like I said, *I* don't know what it's like when it's smoked."

"You must not know who you're talking too."

A failed chemist. I raise my shoulders and drop them.

"I got this." Katrina whispers when Jerry slowly walks past the kitchen.

I've been standing here alone too long with his woman. I'm sure he's probably wondering what we are up to or how she's doing.

To my surprise, Katrina seems at ease. I lived long enough to know what type of drug person is on from their reaction. Someone high on weed using has this vacant gaze in their eyes and something edible in their hand. They still have motion to their body, but it's dialed down a notch. Someone amped up on stronger paraphernalia like crack is all over the place. Katrina, on the other hand, is progressing as if she is simply going along with the movement of her body. She's speaking to me as she dumps the leaves from the basket into a trash bag. Talking about how to get over some of Jerry's clients like pinch a little off their stems or give them dud bags (as if I'm not one of those schmoes. That's how I know her guard is down). I wouldn't have been able to fully focus on de-seeding a plant, talking, and cooking at the same time, but in her case every step she takes or a raise in her hand seems automated. She's been doing this far too long.

"What are your plans." I question.

"Cook it up and pass out free baggies."

"Free?"

"Yeah." Katrina nods her head and hands me a single leaf that way I know what to pluck. "If they like it, then I know you struck oil. If you're going back to the garden, be sure to grab more. Here's your basket."

I nod my head. Katrina then digs into her little handbag and pulls out a small baggie. She hands it to me, and I see it's some of her best stash for my mom. "It's on the house."

"Thanks."

"By the way." Katrina steps a bit closer to me that way I could hear her as she talked in a low tone of voice. "You're looking well." She reaches over my head and runs her fingers through my hair. "Must be making a change for your new girlfriend."

"New girlfriend?"

"Yeah. That woman in the forest you were telling me about. What's her name?"

"Nancy."

CHAPTER SEVEN

Hope

I didn't have the opportunity to talk to her long enough to learn her name, but something about Nancy is befitting for the woman in the garden. Natural all the way, earthly, and pure. I can't recall seeing a blemish on her face or through the sheer cloth over her nude body and I can't stop my mind from reminiscing on the way she walked through the garden. The bottom of her feet had no dirt on them as if she was lightly hovering over the ground by an inch.

In another woven basket, she tossed seeds with her eyes forward, faithful they'd land where she wanted to. I wonder how she was able to live naked in the forest and be one with nature. Only weird, preservationist freaks looking to get back into tune with how God originally made them would do that and many would collapse within minutes without their new aged societal conformities kicking in like a caffeine fiend.

Nancy is natural with it, almost inhuman and I had to know more about her. I'm longing to go back to rest my head on her lap and listen to the music of the wild. Singing birds, the waterfall coming from the skies splashing into the pond, the cool air as it drove past my ears in soft whispers. Somehow, after eating the plant, I finally felt calm and free from the failures in my life that sat in my face day and night. The eyes, however terrifying, after a while I could possibly get past them and live there forever. Maybe…if it was all real and not some hallucination.

I make it home just as the clock on the radio strikes five and frown at the sight of the evening sun slowly disappearing behind the row of houses to the east leaving the sky stained with a mixture of violet and deep ocean blue. I can already hear my mother nagging me for taking too long, but commuters returning home from their dead-end corporate jobs were congesting the roadways.

I ended up driving through the back roads again with my head nearly out the window as I looked around for a mark I left behind. It was still there, a slice of my jacket tied against a branch on a tree, and I hoped no one would take it off. Without it, I won't know where to begin and from that point from to walk straight in the direction that guy told me to go. Any specific landmark I had remembered was the start of the pond where the land got soggy and that terrifying wall of void crawling up in the horizon the closer, I get to it.

Before I can even put my key in the lock, Carol opens it and steps outside the house. Her brows are knitted in a frown, and she folds her arms across her chest.

"*Where have you…*" She shouts but catches the tone of her voice and lowers it upon realizing Roger is still sleeping in the living room. "Where have you been?"

A grin stretches across my face as I hand her the tiny bag containing her "medication".

"I've been out."

"Getting your hair done I see." She points to my scalp. "Is that a wig?"

I comb my fingers through my hair. God, it feels amazing to do that. "Nah."

"Hair plugs?" Carol guesses again. I laugh, shake my head, and move past her into the house. What I desperately need is a hot shower. There's a tickling in my sack and not in the good way. It feels like ants are crawling all over my junk. Anyways, she probably wouldn't believe me if I told her what happened.

Like I thought, Roger is passed out on the living room sofa. The room faintly glows from the television still running on the same twenty-four-hour news broadcast.

The regular reporters update their viewers on the upcoming weather that has yet to change and wont until spring is over. Oncoming rain over and over in different ways of saying it. Showers, downpour, storms. I don't recall it raining in the garden despite there being a massive circular clearing of trees. But then again, that strange cloud was hovering over the pond.

When I finish my shower after finally flushing my stomach of everything, I meet my mother out on the back porch. She's already puffing away on her wrapped skunk smelling stick and feeling its calming effects.

I sit down ajar from her in a black camping chair while she sits in her red one and examine her appearance, unchanged from this morning. I gaze at her fingers not gently wrapped around the joint but locked in different positions. She hasn't been able to fully flex her fingers without feeling a burst of pain in a while. For this smoke break, she's pushing past the ache.

My eyes move to the beaded plant between the fingers of my right hand and a bowl of ripe strawberries I picked up on the way home in my other hand.

The pain I woke up to this morning isn't as noticeable right now. But it's coming back. That I expect from taking any type of drug unless I remain in the water and constantly am consuming the plant. The temporary natural bliss of feeling weightless from all emotional and physical turmoil is worth it and it's something I want to give to my mother.

I hope happiness washes over her as it did Katrina and I.

I hand her the plant and the bowl of fruit. "Eat this."

"I already ate."

"Just try this." I urge and push the plant into the palm of her hand.

She chews down on the plant and strawberry.

I don't know if it was the beads or the firmer center of the fruit, but I hear her teeth crunch down on something and watch her mouth twist into disgust until she swallows everything down and gags.

"What the hell was that?" Carol asks, coughs, and chugs a gas station plastic cup-her favorite-full of water.

She continues to cough and even gags, spits a seed out and leans forward while wrapping her arm around her stomach.

Feeling my heart hammering against my chest, my eyes grow wide, and I lean close to her. This isn't the reaction I expected. I apologize over and over again with one foot stretched ahead of the other and my ass partially raised from the chair. Intuition is screaming at me to get my mother to the hospital, damn Roger if I have to leave him behind, but she reaches out for me to sit and finished off what's left in her cup.

"That was awful." My mother says and shivers. "Where

did you get that?"

"There was a farmers market downtown." I say and see her eyebrow raise. She's been living in this bleak town well past my current lifetime. On her countless visits through what little is offered in the community, there's never been a stand or a bench holding produce from homegrown gardeners. Hell, what's offered in the grocery store is damn near rotting as if Greenwood gets the last picking of produce.

I could've said I got it from there, but the lie is already set in motion and seeing my mother return to her joint as if I gave her nothing sparks an eagerness to keep it going. Would she believe me?

Hell no. To lie is better.

"I got a job." I say with a quick glance at her.

"Oh yeah?" She takes another inhale, skeptic. "Congratulations. Where?"

"Gardening for a private farmer."

My mother takes one last puff on her joint and puts it out in her makeshift aluminum foil ashtray. "That's good." She says and coughs. "That means you're on the right path. What's your plans after that? You're going to start saving. Get your own place. Come by and visit me once every three months-

"Whoa" I chuckle. "You're thinking way too far into the future, ma. And I won't cut myself from you like that."

I lean over the arm rest of the chair and kiss her on the cheek. It makes her entire face turn rose red, and she blessed me with a yellow snaggle-tooth smile. She doesn't want me to leave, which probably angers Roger. Without me in the house to stop her from doing every one of his commands, she'd be under his total control. I'm also someone she can talk to openly.

"I'm happy for you, baby. I can already see the change in you." Carol says. "You don't look so tired. It's like I'm looking at you thirty again."

The pond. I start to feel the chair rocking back and forth as a memory flashes before my eyes. That guy I was carrying. Him laying out in the middle of the road leaking a pool of blood from his scalp and had a twisted leg. I shudder. The kind of quake to the body where it really does stir your soul as if someone with big feet is dancing over your grave. And somehow, I still feel the cringing effect of hearing him snap his bones back into place, the rumble of his body rolling over the roof of my car. The screech of my tires against the pavement when I tried to avoid him.

Carol rests her hand on my shoulder and asks if I'm alright. I seemed to have gone out on her, blankly staring at the concrete patio floor as she was saying something.

"Yeah." I answer standing up. "I'm going to lay down."

I analyze myself in the bathroom mirror and notice my pupils have gone back to their normal pea sized shape, but my eyes are bloodshot as if I hadn't slept in days. I'm starting to feel exhausted, the weight under my eyes-the luggage of my lifespan-is getting heavier. The entire day took a lot of energy from me in every area of my existence. Yet, I feel untroubled, almost like I can grab something to eat, roll into bed, and pass out without wondering what the next day would bring me. Still, a thought in the back of my mind keeps crawling forward, digging its nails into the tissue of my brain.

I killed someone.

My right hand starts to tremble. When I clubbed that man, I felt the vibration of the rock meeting his head from my fingers to my wrist. I don't know what happened to me. Why did I continue to hit him after that? It was as if suppressed rage had finally seen an opening within me and quickly emerged out of my body. I continued to batter the rock down because I was pissed. I went through the trouble of helping him out when I should have thrown him in the back seat of my car and drove him to the nearest hospital.

I listened to him. I took that chance to follow his bewildering request. I dragged him on my shoulder through that forest. What the hell was I thinking? I should have driven off from the start. There weren't any cars on the road that would have seen me anyways. Maybe that is why I can sleep peacefully now. After he tried to kill *me*.

But if I did drive off, I would've never met Nancy and got a glimpse of a world so majestic, far beyond my comprehension and a shining light into this melancholy world I'm stuck in.

I grip my aching chest and force back the tears coming up in my eyes. I have to be strong for myself and my mother. I can't let her down now that I continued on the train of this lie, especially when it makes her happy.

I make myself a peanut butter sandwich and eat it in the dark kitchen with a glass of milk.

As I creep to my bedroom, I take a quick glance in the living room to find my father snoozing on the sofa. It's the only time he is at peace even though it's a heavily medication slumber. He will definitely wake up groggy, thirsty and irritable in the morning, but resting for now, he can't see what is happening in the world he is too terrified to go out into now that his legs don't work.

Sound asleep, He doesn't see my mother in her sadness and yell at her for not making *him* feel better all because his situation is worse. Resting, he doesn't have me to look at either. A failure of a son.

My father wanted me to follow his footsteps into the army and make something better out of it and myself, but I chose to stay home and chase after my own lofty dream. He knew it wasn't going to bloom the way I wanted and when he returned home paralyzed with a broken mindset to find me laying in my messy bedroom watching cartoons, that was it. His hatred for me became unchangeable. I could have a real job, and he'd still insult me in some way.

My eyes shift to the television where the same bullshit from this morning continues to play. God, I want to throw this tv out the window and make sure he never gets another one.

I make a mental note to leave before he wakes up around five-thirty. Carol will tell him I got a job and had to start early in the morning.

Sneaking past her bedroom, I stop to glance through the space between the door and the frame. She's folding clothes while watching tv. A steam of smoke raises from another cigarette that is placed on the nightstand. She takes a puff, softly laughs to not wake her husband and continue folding clothes.

When I make it to my bedroom and flipped the light switch on after closing the door, I instantly feel cool air floating into the open space through a crack in the window and smell pine-sol.

Carol cleaned my room. She made my bed, dusted the tables and television, and is now folding my washed clothes.

What would I do without my mother? What will she do without me? I'm her only child. A last burst of happiness in her dimming world. But I have to leave it. I had to go back to the forest. There's an urge to go back not because of the woman or the plants. I murdered someone and I have to get rid of the body.

I sigh deeply and run my fingers through my hair. "I'll do it in the morning."

It's too dangerous to go out at night. As I pull my fingers away, I feel a few snaps at my scalp. I looked down at my hand. A startling amount is entangled between my fingers and my hand itself is showing signs of age again. The brown spots are on the back of my wrist.

CHAPTER EIGHT

Dream

Before dawn the next morning, I tip-toe out of my bedroom, through the living room where Roger is still sleeping, and into the kitchen.

I can't find the money Carol had given me yesterday. I must have left it in my pants pocket at Jerry's house and with Katrina washing them, that money is gone into her wallet as service fee.

Through the dimness of the kitchen, I'm able to locate my mother's fanny pack placed on the counter. It pains me as I carefully unzip the largest pouch, like someone is forcing the tips of my fingers into a bowl of acid. There's a wad of cash all ranging from fives to fifties.

Roger has been receiving checks from the government for many years. My mother told me in secret how she goes to the nearest check cashing place after standing for minutes near the post box waiting for the deliverer and she never allows him to see the amount written on the rectangle certified script. When the amount is large, she takes five percent out and hides it for a rainy day. He tells her to use most of the money to pay bills and buy food since she and I aren't working. I assume that is another reason why he's vexed with my presence whenever I come around.

The ticking antique wall clock reads five-fifteen. I slip out of the house, lock the door, and step away from the clearing to be suddenly pelted by thick droplets of rain. Perfect. Just what I need to make to make this mission more challenging. Cold and wet.

I wrap my arm around my stomach and embrace the familiar oncoming pain of two rocks bouncing off the walls of my gut. The urge to go back inside and wince this ache away is strong, but something is pulling me to my car. A thought nagging me like a mosquito in the dark.

My car rattles as I rotated the key into the ignition at least four times.

"Shit." I leaned back in my seat and growl through clenched jaw.

God knows what he's doing and is having a jolly good time messing me.

Not only is my stomach twisting and turning, now my head has a little drummer inside of it. I'm so tired, but I have to go. There's another pull that is outweighing this fearful need to cover my wrongdoing. I can't think straight without thinking 'eat'. I want to feel the grittiness combined with the sweet slushy texture of the prune around my tongue and fall into the effects from the plant. To be back in that sense of calmness like a recovering alcoholic ending a stressful day by cuddling with a bottle of hard liquor. An ineffable relief. Better than sex.

Soon I'll be back resting on Nancy's soft thighs.

The joints of my fingers ache and rattle as I grip the

steering wheel.

When I pull myself forward, I feel a *pop* in my lower spine that burns seconds after.

I turn the key into the ignition once more and heave a sigh of relief when it decides to turn over. The only stop I have to make is to the supermarket about ten miles out of Greenwood into the next town. Surprisingly it's open and the parking lot is empty.

I grab what I need and gawk at the cashier as she scans a shovel, flashlight, duct tape, rope and bottle of water in case I get thirsty. One of her eyebrows is raised high and she's hesitant on taking the cash.

Yeah, I'm going to do exactly what she's thinking. As if I can't look any more suspicious, I tell her to keep the change and damn near run out with the loot to my car.

Dawn is creeping over the horizon of trees, and the damp road is strangely empty of drivers and pedestrians.

I glance at the clock. The time is six-twenty-nine and focus my eyes back on the softly orange tinted road illuminated by the rising sun and my dimming car lights.

Greenwood, Montana is a sleepy sort of town. When it's time for the lights to go out, everyone returns indoors almost like a school bell ringing at dismissal. At five in the evening, all business establishments close and so do all communal activities. Sure, there are a few bars in the town. I think maybe two where everyone knew each other, however they shut down at one in the morning.

I pass by one of two gas stations and notice it's deserted. Not even a clerk can be seen standing behind the register through the dirty windows. A sense of uneasy washes over me as I take a right turn down the back road.

Something's off.

It's still raining, but lighter from when I left home. My busted from age window wipers scuff the shield slowly, back and forth until I grow uneasy at the sound of rubber dragging against glass and turn them off.

Turning onto the back roads, I ease my foot off the gas pedal and drive sluggishly while sticking my flashlight out of the window. It is nearly impossible to find the strip of my jacket amongst the hundreds of thousands tree trunks, fallen branches, and leaves and barely any light. Add the rain and it's like looking for a fucking needle in a haystack. Eventually I find the torn leather just as I'm about to drive off the side of the road.

I pull over, grab the items from the supermarket, and climb out of the car. My knees are knocking together and the flashlight in my hand is shaking. I feel like a fish being pulled on a lure into the depths of the forest, but I'm terrified of coming up on that wall. I know it's nothing but a hedge of dark green leaves and branches bundled so tightly together, yet I can't shake the dread of walking up to something my mind sees as an absorbing force.

It triggers a centipede to go up my spine to where I have to back away from it before I'm pulled in.

I take a deep breath and start moving. A whisper in my mind tells me to keep going straight. I don't remember being directed to make turns through the trees. What I do remember is the cracking sound of the guy repositioning his bones back into place. I shudder and grip the flashlight tighter.

Who exactly was that fucker and why was he that important to the woman? Yeah, it could have been her husband, but then again for all I know it could have been her brother although besides their skin tone they didn't have any resembling features.

I wave the flashlight around from side to side while keeping my footing straight. Before, I didn't really pay any mind to it because my thoughts were on the extreme unbelievable circumstances of dragging the man through the woods, however I'm more cautions now of my surroundings. I'm in moose, bear, and mountain lion domain. The only weapon I have is a shovel and the flashlight to beat the shit out of one if it so happens to see me as breakfast.

Each pace is careful as I remain mindful that each sound of a snap is coming from me stepping on dead leaves and twigs. I stop every so often to listen to the sound of nature. The birds are beginning to sing as the morning continues to rise. The leaves rustle with each gust of wind that blows. It finally stopped raining, thank God, but droplets of water continue to roll off leaves from up above and fall down onto my head and shoulders like a dog shaking itself dry.

I can't stand the thought of being wet again. Before I left out, I packed a bag of spare clothes and placed them in a Zip-lock bag. Hopefully when I submerge underwater (if the garden really exists and it all wasn't just a figment of my imagination) the bag will be sealed tight enough to keep the water from the pond out.

I stop, bend down, and run my fingers against a damp mound of dirt. Unfortunately, since the rain fall, I can't tell if I'm inching closer to that steam or nowhere near it. The only indication I have to rely on at this point is the decomposing body of the man that's if I ever find him or the line of darkness growing higher the closer, I get to it.

Sighing deeply, I stand up straight and suddenly hear a noise behind me. A snap of a twig that wasn't caused by me. Damn, I feel like total shit. My head hurts, my joints are throbbing, and the abrupt adrenaline burst does nothing but make me dizzy as I spin around in complete disorder to look with the flashlight.

I wave it around. The circular beam of light bounces off thick tree trunks and thinning bushes. I continue to hear the snapping sound and wonder if the artificial light that I'm creating is doing nothing but luring curious beast in my direction. I flick the switch off and pray nature's light helps lead me the rest of the way and what remains of the night conceals me.

Standing alone in the fading darkness, I squint my eyes to clear my vision and look deeply into the forest behind me. The noise has stopped, but according to my senses it was loud enough for me to determine its distance. Maybe about twenty feet away from me.

Snap.

That one came directly in front of me.

The sound goes off and I nearly take a leap backward with the shovel now gripped tight in my sweaty hands. A wild animal. It knows I'm here. I know it's close by. My heightened sense of fear causes my body to tremble; every pore seeps out beads of sweat. My ears raise to catch another sound as my eyes fall on everything round me. The trees go on as far as my vision can reach, gazing back at me with grins etched sideways up the texture of their natural form.

Through the branches above me, I catch sight onto scraps of the dark blue sky. I need it to be a bit brighter in order for me to see more. Christ, anything other than trees. I need to spot that wild animal camouflaged within its surroundings in order to continue on with caution. Whether it's a mountain lion, a deer, or raccoon, the least I can do is chase it off with my weapon, but I see nothing while hearing more branches breaking.

I pull the flashlight close to my chest and exhale deeply to calm my heart. "It's all in my head."

The very act of what I'm doing is enough to create panic within me. The fear of being caught burying a body has me on high alert. It's nothing but wild animals and they are not what I should be fearing at the moment. I need to get this over with.

"It's all in my head." I whisper again.

"Hi."

A woman!

I spin around and gasp. Distorted faces of women absently cry out and blood-soaked hands reach out to me through the void wall.

I open my mouth to scream, but the air in my lungs is sucked out of my body.

As nothing comes out, there's an incredible pain in my chest as if something has gripped the inners of my ribcage and is pulling them apart.

****

RRRIIIIIINNNG.
RRRIIIIIINNNG.
RRRIIIIIINNNG.
RRRIIIIIINNNG.

My eyelids tear apart and I release that locked in scream from my dreams. The pain, shit! It's still here.

I wrap my arms around my torso and draw my knees to my chest. My jaw pops and I clench my teeth together and count to however long it takes for me to endure a horrid pain circulating around in my stomach. It feels as if someone had stabbed me through my belly button and is sadistically twisting the blade in my gut.

I bury my face into my pillow, call on the good Lord's name, and curse him for not stopping the phone from ringing in the kitchen. I hear Rogers muffled voice through the door shout something and my mother's hard strides into the location where the noise was coming from.

"Wait a damn minute!" Carol shouts.

The phone stops ringing after the second attempt. I listen to her speak with a raspy dry-throat voice and seconds later she comes into my room. I raise my head from my pillow and shake away the agony that's probably smeared all over my face to keep my mother from worrying. It's bad enough Roger is now awake.

Pieces of her hair are in rollers. She has on her favorite red plaid night gown and for some strange reason, her old ballerina shoes all tied up like in her old professional days.

"Someone is on the phone for you." Carol says.

I groan and drop my head down. "Who?"

"Some girl."

"CAROL!" Roger shouts, then spits out a few curse words.

My mother shoots me with a look of sheer annoyance and slams the door shut.

I grab the phone on my nightstand, remembering a long time ago how I broke the ringer to keep anyone calling from waking me up.

"Shut up!"

Roger howls in pain and there's a heavy thump from the living room.

"Christ. What the hell is wrong with them?" I mutter and shove the phone up to my ear.

"Hey." Katrina says with a voice full of giddy and attentiveness. My heart leaps over a beat. I glance at the clock on my nightstand and see it's a quarter to five in the morning. Why the hell is she calling at this time? "Did you happen to grab anymore of those plants?" She questions.

"Do you know what time-

"When are you planning on going back?"

I scoff. "I don't know. Tomorrow in the morning."

"Can you go now?"

I sit up in bed still feeling the horrid pain in my stomach. My esophagus then tightens up as I feel a ball of acid travel upward into my mouth. I drop the phone, throw my hand over my mouth, and dash towards a small steal trash bin at the corner of my room. Through the receiver, Katrina is calling out my name as I'm vomiting up tiny balls of yellow goo. I keep gagging, but nothing is coming out now that my stomach is empty. I don't understand. I didn't eat anything except a sandwich.

I crawl back to my bed but remain on the floor and lean on the edge of the mattress. I can't be far from the garbage at the risk of throwing up again. Also, every joint in my body is throbbing. My knees feel as if I was crawling a mile through a concrete enclosed bunker. My ankles ache and my knuckles burn like I had been digging a hole in wet sand for hours. Trying to get back in bed will be the equivalent to climbing up a mountain at my age on a poor diet.

"GENE! HELLO!"

I snatch the phone from my bed and growl, "I told you I wasn't going back until the morning. What the fuck is wrong with you?"

"If you're not going back like *right now* then at least tell me the exact spot on the back trail so I can go there."

My eyes expand as I catch onto an idea. It's early in the morning and Katrina is calling me. Never before had she done so. Jerry is the only person who did on rare occasions, and I don't hear him shouting at her in the background for speaking to another man so late.

"Where are you?" I ask.

"Outside on a pay phone. I have Jerry's car." She answers almost like she knew the next questions I was about to ask.

Hearing this, despite the pain I'm experiencing, I jump to my feet and nearly stumble over on my bed. I catch myself on the edge and suddenly yelp when I see that my sheets are covered with my hair. I touch the crown of my head and stagger at the smoothness of my skin.

"Gene!" Katrina shouts through the receiver. "Hello. Hello. Can you tell me where that place is?"

My damn hair is gone, my skin feels like one of my mother's worn out, off brand leather bags, and the pain in the pit of my stomach is back. Through my sudden frantic reaction, the exhaustion of my age swiftly returns. I can't stand for long without feeling tremendously weak and not in control of the world spinning underneath me. I bite down on my tongue and try not to curse at the top of my lungs. From the next room I hear Roger already shouting at my mother to rotate him on the sofa. I don't want to stir her mind any further than it already is.

"I don't remember." I say into the phone. Katrina growls on the other end. "What happened with the stash in the bag?"

"It's gone."

"WHAT? How? You just cooked it." I say while slowly climbing back into bed.

"I was giving out free baggies to test and word got around. Everything was gone in about three hours."

I hear Jerry say something along the lines of 'he's got to get more' like he's in the car shouting at his girl. I pull the phone away from my ear in disbelief. They're together? He sounds way too excited like her and that makes me extremely nervous. I'm not a fan of being urgently needed for something. Especially over a matter that is really beyond my comprehension. Part of me thinks the forest could've been a dream. I mean, come on. A talking wolf and swan beside a nude woman. The only confirmation of their existence is my friends need of what grew there. This is all real.

I stay on the line silent, listening to Katrina's heavy breathing and the sound of thunder rolling on the other end. She then calls out to me and my name echoes throughout my mind mixed with beats of my own thoughts. I too want that feeling to return. The euphoria of youth. However, I don't want them to have any access to it.

"I can't remember where it was." I say with an exaggerated sigh. "I'll have to drive around and see-

"You didn't leave a marker?" Katrina asks. "Like a shirt around a tree."

"Hey! I said I don't know. It's late. I'll call you when I wake back up." I slam the phone down on the receiver and go into the kitchen for a glass of water. My mother glances up at me from a bowl of soft food she was mixing with a wooden spoon. I can see behind the smoke that rose from her cigarette, she is carrying bags of exhaustion under her bloodshot tiresome eyes.

"Can you take this to your dad." She hands me the dish that smells like maple syrup and cinnamon.

I scoff. "Why are you cooking him food this early?"

"Christ, Gene." Carol rubs the bridge of her nose. "Just give him the damn food before he starts yelling."

Plopped in his wheelchair in front of the television playing the twenty-four-hour news cycle, my father frowns upon my arrival from the kitchen. His hands are shaking faster and harder than normal. He moves his gaze around me when

I put the oatmeal down as if I'm blocking his view of the same shit that was just spoken over twenty minutes ago. The annual celebration of a meteor, predictions of oncoming war, and the rise of childbirth. Cold and gloomy Montana weather as the season changes from winter to spring. What is something new to be said?

"She's in there acting like a real bitch." Roger snarls.

I walk away without saying a word but can feel the sharp stare of my dad like hot rays beaming through my flesh and into my spine. When I return to the kitchen, slipping my jacket on, my mother has another cigarette lit over a cup of coffee. Steam rises from the surface, mocking her with a familiar dance she could no longer do. She rubs the back of her neck and sighs hard looking my way.

"Sorry about that." I say and gently rub her back.

She nods and pulls the cigarette from between her lips. "Are you going to get more of that plant you gave me?"

Again, my heart skips a beat. Her too?

She looks me up and down, seeing that I'm dressed and smiles. "Off to work?"

"Yeah. I'll try to be back as soon as possible."

Carol frowns but quickly turns around. She doesn't say anything else to me, nor looks my way and it pains me to leave her behind, but I have to make a move before the sun rises, and Jerry finds the marker.

I kiss her on the cheek and scoop my car keys from the counter.

CHAPTER NINE

Return

I check up and down the street, as far as my eyes could see, for Jerry's red Thunderbird. He's smart on the mischievous side and if I struck gold, he'd want to know for himself where I got it. No middleman. I can see myself being beaten to death at the pond by my acquaintance. Maybe not beaten with a rock but tormented with the butt of their guns until I reveal the access point into the garden.

The guy's bloodied face suddenly flashes before my eyes, and I grip the steering wheel feeling my stomach crumble into a knot. Good thing I didn't eat anything. The memory of his scent, blood and sweat fills my nostrils and I gag.

I can't believe I killed someone.

It's an action I cannot shake from my consciousness no matter how bizarre the situation was that led to it. On my right shoulder, there's a whisper telling me the bastard deserved what came to him, if not I would be the one sinking into the earth with festering flesh overtime. On my left, more whispers tell me I had no right to take a life. Damn my human nature and its need to survive. Damn myself for not driving away from the start.

I take the same road and drive under thirty in a sixty mile per hour road.

Before leaving, I grabbed a flashlight out of the garage since it's still dark. My faint headlights-in need of a clean and bulb change-can brighten so far down the road. Looking to my left while driving will strain my eyes.

I shift my eyes from forward to my left every two seconds as to not miss my marker and every so often, I glance into the rear-view mirror for any cars, especially Jerry's. A torn piece of my jacket is wrapped around the base of a small tree amongst its towering counterparts. Once I see it, I pull my car over to the side of the road a few feet ahead to throw Jerry off just in case.

I swing my gaze at every direction to be absolutely certain no other cars are coming up both sides of the road and start on the straight path into the woods extremely exhausted with a black basket in my hand.

What if it was all a dream? No. It had to be real. I have all the evidence I need to prove that there are other dimensions hidden within this world, possibly behind several thick walls that to the bare eye from afar, looks like a void. That terror of seeing something unknown is sure to keep people from exploring out of fear.

On the other side of these walls, they all have beautiful women in fields of fruit and vegetables. It's absurd to think that, but it calms my nerves as I tread through the forest alone. Despite him being busted up and trying to attack me, that guy's presence was comforting. By myself, I hear every snap of a twig caused by wildlife. The fallen leaves crunch into pieces under my feet. My breathing is heavy and short from exhaustion and fear. Just keep straight, is all I have to do.

Ten minutes in, I hear something. Like someone with a raspy dry throat is breathing with their mouth open.

"Gene." A faint whisper of a woman. I spin around with the flashlight in the air. Fuck. Not this again. Blinking several times proves this isn't a dream.

I pick up the nearest thick branch and cry out "Who's there?"

A cackle from an animal responds like an alarm that triggers more to shout out. I can't determine what creature it might be. A bird like a vulture, monkey? It sounds like a witch's laughter that brings a strange feeling that there's many eyes on me, yet I haven't even made it to the damn garden yet. My skin bubbles with goosebumps and I tremble feeling a cold shift in the once dense air.

Slow steps backwards, with the stick raised in the air, I've never been more vigilant in my life, fearful, and also ready to attack. The act of murder and getting away with it does something to one's psyche. My possibilities have become limitless as long as I don't get caught and either Jerry or Katrina, for this secret I'm willing to break a piece of lumber across their skulls.

My right foot sinks into the earth and from my heel to my toes, my socks soak up the warm water of the opening. I turn around, giddy until my breath is sucked away by the terrifying edge of nothingness. My heart makes a single hard beat and blood from adrenaline rushes throughout my skull. I let out a cry and take quick steps backwards as my eyes adjust to the void wall. My mind screams not to touch it, even though in reality, it's a hedge of dark green leaves. Ones you'd see in an affluent neighborhood where riches demand privacy.

So, why is it frightening?

There's no reflective shimmer of the pond underneath it. Although the sun is coming up, shining through the leaves above me, the void swallows its rays. Without squinting my eyes, there's no definition, no textures or shadows between the leaves. Without color or form, I don't understand it and the heaviness of the air feels draining the closer you get.

The garden is on the other side where the trees peeing over the towering hedge are morphing like caterpillars moving behind the fog. Once my mind has settled and I get use to the wall, I toss my weapon to the side and lean over the glistening water. It's so clear I can see the brown earth with specks of diamonds. I fish out a couple and stuff them in my pants pocket, mindful to take them out when I get to my car and put them in a cup I saved from the gas station.

When I dip my hands into the water, I feel my skin tightening especially around my eyes where the luggage was becoming too heavy to bear. Any longer, I probably would've passed out due to exhaustion. I smile as the marks of age and abuse to my poor limbs fade and my entire body becomes warm and loose like a noodle being cooked. I've truly discovered the fountain of youth.

A soft wind blows and the trees above me shake their heads.

"Hey." Someone whispers.

Who the hell is it!

I spin around and look everywhere, but it's hard to see a person amongst thousands of sycamore legs.

I kneel down and reach for something to use as a weapon. I threw my stick too far and my ears are already perked up to lose focus on what is around me. Every little sound matters, a footstep, heavy breathing, hell, jeans rubbing together at the thigh.

Finally, my hands touches something with mass, but mushy. Raised before my eyes, I yelp, fling it out of my hand, and stumble back at the sight of a brown arm severed from a torso. The stiff I left behind. The flesh where the arm meets the shoulder is jagged as if wildlife tore it from the body. However, what animal would rip off an arm without taking a bite into the wing?

Remains of the body are still together, the face caved in from the rock and my boot with a swarm of insects forming a kingdom in his eye sockets. I gag at the rancid scent of shit and hard metal, but nothing comes up except bile that burns my throat. The least I could do is give the guy some respect since he did show me to this place. I gather twigs and a pile of dead leaves and throw them over his body.

"Gene." Someone faintly says my name. Soft female voice. Katrina?

I refrain from calling out, holding in my gasp, and continue to move backwards into the pond. My jeans pull in the water like a sponge. I keep my eyes moving all around me and my hand searching the muddy bottom of the pond for the rock that was glued to the surface. I assume that's the only way I'll gain entry to the hidden world.

A massive branch cracks as if a monkey leaped from one tree to another and the witch's laughter sounds off again.

What the fuck is that?

My heart slams against my chest and I clench my jaw together to keep from yelling out in a panic. Finally, my thumb and index finger pull on a stone, but it doesn't budge. I found it!

I hold my breath, sink into the warm, clear water and

reach to confirm this is it. A clear film as thick as arctic ice keeps my fingers from breaking through the surface. I swish my body around for a moment to take in the consuming relief of my aching joints, pain of age melting away. I feel my lungs strengthen as well as my legs and I kick forward to the light at the end of the tunnel.

The swim takes longer than expected. I swish my legs up and down at a slower pace to get a stronger push until the crown of my head knocks up against a wall of dirt, where the earth above begins. I dig my fingers into the ground, pull myself up and out on my belly. The first inhale of air is sweet. Instead of the cackling on the other side, birds sing a morning tune and flutter across the sky.

I exhale and lay on my back to regain some energy. The sun blazing through a clearing between leaves is warm and relaxing. I close my eyes, toss the basket to the side and thank God for the existence of this place. It's real and I feel at home.

"I can live here." I whisper, open my eyes and scream in horror.

The large eyed monster dashes up to me and crouches down.

I'm stuck in dread and hypnosis under its presence and the only thing that keeping me from dying of death is the sweet smell of lemons coming from whatever it is wrapped in a humanoid body.

The monster digs into its basket of fruits and leaves and takes out the prune wrapped in the plant. Like a baby bird, I open my mouth and allow it to shove the food damn near down my throat if I hadn't pulled back to chew. Once it drops to the pit of my empty stomach, things become clearer, brighter, and lighter. Nancy blinks and her eyes change from nothing to normal. Her antlers retract into the bush of her head. Even the trees become less judgmental.

I start to float in my mind as my body sinks into the earth. Nothing matters. None of the shit I have to deal with isn't here. I'm free and back to resting on her thighs.

"Where is the man?" A deep voice snarls at me.

I raise my eyes and lock onto the wolf. His lip twitches and his yellow eyes are fixed on me with a burning glint in his expanded irises. I'm in such a blissful state of mind, I find his hostile demeanor like an angry chihuahua. I hold back laughter and sit up.

"This is all I could find of him." I say and raise the basket.

The wolf barks. He must be able to tell it's a lie. Dogs have a heightened sense of smell, and the stiff isn't too far from here.

Instead, of calling me a liar, the beast snarls and runs its tongue across its fangs.

"Very well, then." It speaks. "I have no option but to use you for the time being."

CHAPTER TEN

Phorix

I walk beside the wolf down a row of lettuce to my right and greens to my left and although I'm used to seeing greenery all around me; of course, from the pines, grass, and bushes of my town, never have I walked through someone's personal garden. And not as marvelous as the one hidden in the forest. Shrubs as tall as I are decorated with a variety of berries, raspberry, blue, and a few patches of strawberry bushes here and there. Lettuce and greens shade me as I pass by and there are trees that line around the pond like loitering humans holding apples, mangoes, and avocados. Strangely, even the wildlife is majestic.

A group of four eyed deer drink from the pond before scurrying off when a flock of swans dive in for a morning swim. The leader of the bunch, the one who showed me the way back, looks over in my direction and cries out a lovely caw. I return the greeting with a wave. The birds are still communicating with one another through high-pitched chirps and tweets. A four eyed fox leaps through the rows of vegetation, stops in the middle of my path to glance at me, and resumes its game of hopscotch.

The wolf stops and sniffs a single plant different from the others. I look and see that it's a steam of beaded leaves. The ones I gave to Katrina. The dog flinches and growls at it. My eyes lock onto five more thick stems spewed in different spots but not far from each other. Jackpot.

"Pull this out of the ground." The wolf commands. He eyes one branch holding the most leaves.

I nod and wrap my fingers around the base of the stem and feel hundreds of sharp jabs in my fingers and palm. I yell, ripping my bloody hand away. The wolf stares at me and sits. "Pull it out."

"Look dammit!" I shout holding up my red-soaked hand.

The dog snarls. "I said remove it."

I rub my hand against my damp shirt to clean the crusting blood from the wounds and look around for Nancy. She's at the pond feeding swans seeds. I'm craving her energy, her presence, smell and touch.

"Tomorrow, I'll pick them." I mumble and place the basket down. "I need gloves."

I take a single step towards her and the wolf leaps in my way.

"Unsuitable human. Only creatures like you have no ill-will against straying from the natural order." The wolf barks and hunches with its tail stiff. "Pull the weeds."

I narrow my eyes and focus my gaze on the dog's stance. He's in a position to attack me with the glare of rage. Like a mother protecting her baby. I can't believe I'm talking to a dog. Well...I hear his voice in my head as if he's a human. Part of me feels like I can kick him to the side like any other mutt. I have the strength to do it. However, my better self says not to battle against a wild animal half my size with multiple lines of sight.

Dropping down to my knees, I keep my gaze on him and suck up the pain in my hands. The weed crunches as I yank hard at the base and rip it out of the ground, roots and all. A river of blood starting at the center of my palm drips down my wrist and I move onto the next weed.

"So." I start to speak. Talking helps to distract the feeling of micro thorns sticking into my flesh. "Tell me about this place. Do others know about it?"

The wolf licks his right paw. "No." The other paw gets cleaned. "You are the only one able to cross the threshold."

"The hedge?" I toss the third branch into the basket and embrace my throbbing hand against my chest.

"How did you get through the threshold?"

"The pond." I answer and rip up another plant.

"Who showed you the way?" The wolf questions.

I wince and hold my burning hand against my chest. He's asking questions and repeating them in my mind the longer I take to answer, like an echo in a canyon. I remember he smelled the guy's blood on me. How else could I have found this place and what lie could I tell him when I returned with the basket?

I stare at the beast, and he looks directly into my eyes. *Who showed you the way?* Nancy comes closer and upon hearing her footsteps into the thick warm grass, the wolf turns away from me to speak to her words I can't hear. It's all in her mind. The perfect time to pull myself together and think of something before he returns back to interrogating me.

"I was out hunting when I found this basket." I say to the wolf, sternly. "I fell into the pond, and this was the only way out of the water or else I would've drowned."

The wolf lowers his head and moans. "No man?"

I shake my head no. "Sorry."

The forest, once pulsing with light and rhythm, is starting to still. The colors that bled together like melted stained glass now dull at the edges. The warmth that once cradled me is fading, replaced with a damp chill clinging to my skin. My vision is sharper, but crueler. I see the trees for what they are: twisted, splintering things. The buzz beneath my skin, that hum of purpose and connection, has gone quiet.

The effects are wearing off.

Suddenly nausea spins through my gut, like my body remembers it doesn't belong here anymore. The harmony I felt with the garden is breaking, splintering like a song cut short. I drop to one knee, clutching my side as dizziness takes over. The wolf doesn't move.

I reach into the basket for a leaf and move it towards my mouth. The wolf suddenly barks and snarls at me. He then leans his head and lets out a soft howl that alerts Nancy like a deer hearing a snap of a twig and she rushes over.

I flinch seeing the darkness back in her large eyes, glittering. It's not an easy sight to get used to no matter how many times I will see her in the future. It's not human.

She takes a leaf from her own basket with another sweet berry and shoves it into my mouth.

"Oh, God." I lay down in the grass and allow my body to float as high as my mind. The void wall doesn't seem so scary the longer I stare at it. Little white dots emerge in the emptiness of it like stars. I reach to graze my fingers along the smoothness of Nancy's foot, but she quickly takes off through the pathway and disappears into the distance. Eventually I will have my body close to hers. For now, my priority is to get back to my world before the effects wear off again. I think I collected enough.

"I have to go home." I say.

"Not until you are finished." The wolf raises its snout in a new direction.

Shit. Without the swan, I won't be able to find my way back and the beast seems like he's the one in command of their forest home.

He finally rests once I yank out the two stems and fling them into the basket. My hand is burning, wet, and sticky, but strangely endurable.

I have to ask. As crazy as it seems, but this is really happening. I have to ask. "Is this Eden?"

The wolf bends its head to the side in an innocent display of confusion. For a second, I feel a strange connection between us, a dog and its owner, having a casual conversation through simple expressions beyond the telepathic weirdness.

"What is that?" It asks.

"A garden. You know, from the Bible. Eden."

"This is a garden, but not the place which you speak of." The wolf finally settles down close to me and continues to speak into my mind. "Before, nothing was here. Until a star fell from the sky and landed in the puddle my pack was drinking from. They made it out before the trees grew. I, however, was trapped with the man and his mate here. I sniffed their bodies up there." The wolf nods towards a thick branch dangling over the pond. My heart skips a beat, and my breathing shortens at the sight of those two nooses dangling in the wind and falling water.

"They never achieved their wishes when the earth changed under their feet. Too terrified until a voice from the pond instructed them to stay and watch over the garden until the true caretaker of it comes. I was ordered to stay and protect them." The wolf wheezes and drops his head down to the earth. "I have failed my part. The order of the garden has been corrupted by your arrival."

I grip the basket and place my hand over my stomach. It's starting to turn along with my vision. I have to eat something more than leaves.

"My hand is killing me." I say and start towards the pond. Nancy, in all her beauty, is picking apples from a tree and I'm craving something from her to chew on. Looking closely, another one instantly grows in its place starting with a core and budding all out into its red sphere-like shape with four little nubs on the bottom. I take one step in her direction, and the wolf is back on my path with it's upper lip raised, baring his teeth, but I'm not frightened. My hand hurts too much for his hostility to matter. "Let me wash the blood off, will you."

It follows and stays at my side as I clean both of my hands off. The water feels like the best masseuse at work between my fingers, over my knuckles, and kneading in the center.

Once my hands are free of blood and the wounds vanish, I pull them out. Far on the other side, Nancy places her basket down and lays flat against the earth to soak up the sun. I stand up straight, glance at the wolf drinking from the water I cleaned my hands in and ponder should I dash towards her while his guard is down.

I don't know where this urgency to touch her came from. I'm guessing it has something to do with the bewilderment of the entire situation I found myself in. On one hand, this still doesn't feel real. On the other hand, it does. It's as if the wolf is standing in the way of a prize I want to have. A trophy if I may say to confirm this garden's entire existence. I want the good leaves and fruit she fed me. I want some of her hair to take back to my world. I want to have her beside me. Not this dog!

"That is all of the weeds." He points his snout in the air and sniffs. "Now, you go back to the other side, and I will resume guard. Be sure that every stem and leaf is burned. Leave no seed behind."

I raise an eyebrow. "What happens if I don't?"

"Calamity will root itself in anyone who consumes the weeds."

"I thought these were good like the ones she gave me!" I shout pointing at Nancy's basket.

The wolf barks. "Burn them! They are the shadow to the light of this garden. The rotten that will taint and choke the others with its corrupted bugs as long as it's here. Order must not fully topple. Burn every last one of them or calamity will grow into wickedness and by then there will be no end to the spreading of Phorix."

****

I pull myself out of the water and find the nearest fallen tree to sit on and ponder. The basket is at my side filled with weeds; specks of my blood are on the stems and leaves. The wolf gave me order to burn them or else something will happen to whoever eats it. How the hell did the stiff burn the weeds? Most likely by rubbing two sticks together and when I ran him over, he was probably in the process of doing so. But why burn something when it makes the eater feel euphoric?

Looking at the weeds now, maybe the beads have something to do with the difference. That, however, I have yet to see. Nothing is making any sense nor does the appearance of the pond.

Of course it's real. I conclude that I stumbled into an alternate world. Ok. Moving on from that realization. He said something about a meteor hitting that location, but being forty, I can't remember that ever occurring and talked about it in the news.

Oh shit.

My eyes grow large, and my pacing slows to a stop right as I'm approaching my car. Roger watching tv. It was mentioned. Something about an anniversary and a meteor that happened *last year*.

I throw the basket in my trunk and decide to go to the public library to calm the racing questions before they collide in my mind and I put myself in an asylum.

CHAPTER ELEVEN

Confirmation

"Excuse me." I whisper to the librarian whose head is buried in a thick book. It takes me two taps on the cold marble counter to get her attention. "Got any newspapers."

She gazes at me past her round glasses with her head still lowered. "We have plenty." She says with a nod to the right. My eyes grow big at the periodical section. Stacks upon stacks of newspapers, although they are neatly arranged, I can't imagine myself flipping through thousands of fragile pages to look for one topic as the final confirmation to a wild story.

"The classifieds are on the top row." The Librarian says.

I scoff and shove my hands into my pocket.

Damn, is it that obvious that I'm without a job? I hate to interrupt her deep dive into another world, but *my* time is of the essence and she's getting paid to read. Might as well take a break and help a fellow.

I lean over the counter and force a smile on my tiring face. The sensation of sagging skin, especially under my eyes and around my jaw, is like ice cream melting in your hands. "I'm looking for a specific topic. Something about a meteor crash here not too long ago."

She finally raises her head and flares her nostrils.

"Astronomers predicted the collision to be world-ending. Maybe half of the land where it was supposed to hit was going to be set on fire," The Librarian says. Her name is Missy, and she smells like lilacs I used to pick off trees in a bundle and run on home to give to Carol. She chuckles, pulls out one bundle of newspaper, and sets it down on a wide Mahogany table.

"I bought myself an extra pair of glasses and chose to work overtime here on the set night. Sadly, nothing happened, and I was out a hundred and fifty dollars." Missy smirks and taps the top headline written in big bold letters LYRA'S COMET: GLOBAL DEVASTATION OR HEAVENS DREAM? Printed 1987.

I raise an eyebrow and try to recall when I heard about this rock or the panic that surrounded it. What exactly was I doing last year? My father was home at the time still watching the 24 hour news station. Or is my life that depressing where my bedroom swallowed me up for majority of the year and all fear surrounding the end of the world was blocked? Did I even care to notice and was ready to end it all like Nancy and her friend-whoever he was to her?

My stomach turns at the recollection of those two nooses dangling from the tree branch.

"Anniversary was a couple of days ago." The librarian says with a sigh. "I use the day to mourn the mass suicide down south. A small community took their lives thinking it was their time to go home before being stuck in hell on Earth.

While Missy continues to talk, I scan the small letters on the fine paper and read upon entering Earth's atmosphere in a massive fiery ball broke. It came down in two areas, one here in Montana and another light was seen way down south, somewhere overseas.

"If I could read all of these books, I would. The crash would've given me more time."

"Mmm." I nod my head and thank her for helping me.

Outside, the road is sleek and the air smells crisp with a bit of heaviness to it as if moisture from the sudden burst of rain was still floating like a fog. I shield my eyes against the glare of the setting sun and check the time on my wrist watch. It's a quarter to six! The day seemed to have slipped past me like a breeze.

I curse under my breath and move faster around a curve in the back of the library, where I parked. A guy is walking around my car. He looks curious, particularly towards my trunk and when he sees me, he grins. Getting close enough to look him in the face, I take a nervous step to the right and keep my gaze on his eyes shifting from side to side rapidly.

"Can I help you?" I ask while shoving my key into the door. The guy is standing on the other side. Hearing me unlock it, he moves around to reach me. I yank the driver's door open, slam it shut and roll down the window to a crack. His eyes continue to rattle. It's fucking weird. They stop when he blinks, but for as long as he keeps his lids apart, his irises start moving like a baby welding a rattle.

"Something smells good in your car." He chuckles and exposes a top row of browning teeth. "You're a dealer?"

This guy is familiar, one of Jerry's top buyers and sometimes I run into him around town or down in the parking lot waiting for Katrina to finish cooking. He never looked this bad, not that I got the chance to speak to him for long, but in passing, his eyes were once normal, and his teeth weren't as yellow like dried mustard. A smell coming from him like piss is nauseating. My nostrils flare and the back of my throat tingles the longer he's nearby. Him, standing so close to my car is making me highly fearful and sick.

I shake my head and turn on the car. "It's flowers."

"Flowers don't smell that sweet. I know you. You're going to Jerry's."

I internally scream and grip the steering wheel tight. Why won't this bozo get out of the way? He's close against my door, almost to where his nose is centimeters away from the space between the cracked window. I'm certain his foot is in position to get run over.

"Come on, man. Don't hold out on me." The guy says. His fingers slip through the slit between door and window and he's using his weight to push it down. I grab the handle and turn it clockwise to bring the window back up, but this guy is steadfast on getting to the bottom of what's in the trunk even if it means shoving down my window by force to reach the latch button.

I turn the key in the ignition and-with sheer luck-my car rumbles to a start. Desperately trying to keep the window from being forced down any further, I yank the gear into reverse and yelp when this fucking weirdo shoves the window down and reaches across my face for the car key.

"What the hell! Stop!"

"I can smell it!"

This man is fucking crazy. Looking at him, he looks like a rabid animal. More terrifying than the wolf. He shows me his teeth pressed tight together with spit oozing from the corners of his lips. Through the blaring rock music playing on ragged speakers, I can hear him snarling like a bear against a moose.

I swing my left arm anywhere the manic is reaching for, between the steering wheel and the key. He holds on as my car swerves in reverse. My heart is pounding against my chest and my legs- due to fear- suddenly loses connection with my brain. I stumble in confusion between the brakes and the gas pedal, shift the gear into drive and slam on the gas.

The asshole holds onto the door and fights for the steering wheel as I'm trying to shove his body out of the car. A quick glance, I see that his eyes are bloodshot, his gums are bleeding, and there's black lines etched on his face like veins, raised underneath his transparent skin. I yell in a panic, and it clicks like a switch. When flight is not helping, fight mode takes over. Instinct takes hold of my entire body and my elbow slams against the man's nose. My car dips into a pothole and that sudden jerk downward throws his grip loose.

I see his body roll in the rear-view mirror and thank God I just so happen to drive down a road that's empty of cars and pedestrians to see what happened.

I drive straight to the gas station, buy a canister and lighter, and fill it to the rim. Enough to consume both weeds and basket in flames to a pile of dust. The only place I can do that without drawing any suspicion is returning to the back roads, but dusk is approaching, and my head is starting to spin in exhaustion and hunger.

Despite being tired, my body hasn't stopped shaking from adrenalin and every second, I turn my gaze over my shoulder. That guy's face was frightening. Yet, I'm not sure if that type of reaction is from the weeds. Maybe Jerry added crack to his inventory and the plants just so happen to smell like rocks. The wolf did order me to burn the plants and after my trip to the library, there's no blaming what I saw on a hallucinations. That world is real. I stumbled into another dimension. A beautiful piece of land where everything is fresh and regenerative.

With shaking hands, I remove an aged weed covered in tiny black beads. Compared to the one Nancy fed me, how could these plants be the opposite of that? But now that I ponder it, everything is contrary to something else.

I drop the plant back into the basket, slam the trunk shut, and run my fingers through my hair. A chunk comes out, brown mixed with gray strands balled up like a tumbleweed. I flinch and nearly shout, but remember it happened the last time. My back starts to ache and my elbow, the one used to knock the guy out, is throbbing. The heaviness of my own body is noticeable along with the liver spots on the back of my hand that seemed to have doubled.

God, I've never felt so exhausted in all of my life. The comedown from that plant is hitting me and its worse this go around. Driving home is dangerous as everything is starting to spin and I can hardly keep my eyes open.

This is the last drop off. I swear. At least Katrina will be happy until the well runs out.

CHAPTER TWELVE

Rooted

I knock once, wait two seconds, knock twice, and cough as loud as possible. It's Jerry's way of knowing I'm on the other side of the door. My pain is unbearable, and a blistering headache is growing behind both of my eyes. Christ, I feel like I'm dying. Even my breathing has shortened, my chest feels heavy, and it burns to breathe in and out. There's a lingering metal taste at the back of my throat from the codeword.

The door flings over and the barrel of Jerry's gun is back in my face.

I hold my hands up, the handle of the basket dangling between my thumb and index finger. "Really man?" I say and push the gun down.

"Right." Jerry chuckles and shoves his gun back into the sleeve at his side. He pokes his head out of the doorway, looks to the right, then left, and gestures me to come inside. With everything happening, I'm craving my own bed. All I need is a couple of Tylenol-which I know Katrina has, a bottle of water, and maybe fifteen minutes for the drugs to work down this awful ache.

"I can't. I just came to drop this off." I toss him the basket. "It's my last run by the way."

He scoffs. "I wasn't asking."

I don't know why I let this little punk get the best of me. He maybe a couple of inches taller than me with more muscle mass, but I'm older and wiser. I can't take him out physically because I'm also out of shape, however I *can* set some authority.

I glare at the kid, straight lips and a raised eyebrow. Jerry returns the same look and opens the door wider.

"Shit." I only step inside because my knees are starting to scream for me to get off of them.

I head straight for the couch and lay down, damp clothes and all. Luckily the furniture is made out of leather, but it stinks like cat piss and makes my head pound harder. I press my wrist against the bridge of my nose and force myself to get past the pain coming at me in hurricane wind waves.

Jerry kicks at my dangling leg and I wince in pain. It's as if he's wearing spikes at the tips of his toes.

"You look and smell like dirt." He says standing over me. "You went back to that spot?"

I sigh and put one of those small decorative pillows over my head. The streetlight directly facing their apartment, shining through the broken blinds, is making my eyes burn. Why does everything hurt! I just want to get home but I fear I'll pass out at the wheel. Is this what old age feels like? Life as a 97-year-old with the grim reaper looming over my shoulders. I've wasted my entire life. A forty year old drug mule in constant pain. I can't live like this. It's better to burn the weeds in the fucking forest and go back to the garden than do *this*. I should've done that from the beginning.

Dammit, I should've drove off!

Something falls onto my lap. I lift the pillow and reach for what rolls down between my legs, a bundle a cash tied together with a rubber band. Looking past it, Katrina quickly ducks off into the kitchen without saying anything to both me and Jerry. The crash of steel and glass sound off and the beeping of her oven turning on follows. I sit up and look at the first bill. A twenty. I wonder if it's just a cover and the rest are singles. Each small baggy of Jerry's weed goes for five bucks. Whoever ordered twenty wanted enough to last.

"That's payment for the next batch." He says taking a seat beside me and runs a hand through his full head of brown hair finally out of braids. I scoff and put the pillow back over my face, envious. The last chunk of my lovely locks fell out as soon as I parked in the lot.

"I'm not going back." I grumble. At least not for these two bozos.

"Then you need to tell us where the garden is, fat ass." Jerry shouts. "You're playing with money here and there's fish hungry for those little flakes you gave us. Now you want to back out just as business is getting started. Got someone else who pays more for it or something?"

"No."

Katrina steps out of the kitchen, giggling and I feel my heart immediately sink into the pit of my gut. She's wearing sunglasses indoors in the night. Her face is turned my way, and I see her jaw shifting from side to side. She acknowledges my presence with a nod and goes to answer a knock at the door with her hand behind her back. She's strapped as well. Jerry wouldn't let her open the door being a woman without a weapon.

She keeps the deadlock latched, opens the door as far as it could go against the piece of metal, and says something in a deep mumble that makes her boyfriend, and I exchange quizzical glances at each other. The person on the other side moves towards the crack and says something more to her. I gasp, chest burning and stomach twisting into a knot. The guy I elbowed raises his eyes from her, directly at me, and grins.

"Hey!" Katrina snaps her fingers to reclaim his attention. "I said I'm not done cooking and don't call this house anymore. You know the fucking deal times." She slams the door on his face and shakes her head with a twisted lip. Jerry laughs at her boldness and throws an arm over the back of the sofa.

"That's my girl."

Biscuit comes out the bedroom, meows and rubs up against her mother's leg. I'm starting to feel uneasy. That guy is definitely going to get revenge in some way after seeing me again and I can't help but to have the same alertness with Katrina. She's covering her eyes. Are they shifting like her buyer? I slowly sit up on the sofa and prepare myself for something to happen. The cat that continues to show its mother love even though it's not reciprocated except glared at in return.

Katrina snatches her cat by the nape and yanks the creature off the ground like a sack of potatoes.

"I told you to stay out of the kitchen." She snarls and chucks poor Biscuit across the living room. I flinch and tense up like I'm the one who took the pain of the throw.

The poor animal crashes into a pile of books and glasses of water resting on top of a flimsy table. The sudden burst of loud noise petrifies that cat and after gaining traction on a sheet of paper, it scurries off to the bedroom. Jerry's mouth hangs open while I'm gripping the pillow, praying it's strong enough to take a bullet, God willing she doesn't take her wrath out on me if she's anything like that guy.

"I'm on my period." She declares and steps up to me. "So., I heard you don't want to play the middle man anymore." Katrina smirks, digs into her apron pocket and pops a single beaded plant wrapped around a grape into her mouth like a piece of gum.

"He doesn't want to tell us where now that business is booming." Jerry adds and slaps my back.

"How do you get here so fast?" Katrina questions.

"I-is your cat alright?" I ask.

"She's fine. Stupid ass nearly burned her paws yesterday when she jumped on the hot stove. Anyways, you said you took the back roads, huh? Into the preserves? I had a dream I was walking through it." Katrina moves her right hand behind her back. "I saw you."

I nervously laugh, sensing heat from her boyfriend besides me. She takes my silence for a clue and smirks.

"Mmm…so it's somewhere in that forest?"

I chew on the side of my mouth and rotate my glances between Jerry and his girl. They must think I'm an idiot if I'm going to give them markers. All I can think about is Nancy and how I left her behind possibly vulnerable. The wolf is with her, yet he's only one animal. He might be against something greater. Not human. It's bewildering to assume that but the laughter I heard in the forest still rings in my mind and that didn't sound like another animal or human. I can't let them touch that place and ruin it for me.

"Guys…" I nervously chuckle and pull the lobe of my ear. "it's not that serious."

Katrina fishes another raw, beaded leaf from her apron and dangles it by the stem, turning it between her fingers with a wide grin smeared on her dry face. "You stumbled on a natural accelerate that gives you this feeling like you can finally live life without fear of consequences and judgment and you're telling me it's not that serious? There's really beauty in this God forsaken place. So much dirt to take root in." She laughs and places the plant on her tongue, slowly moving it into her mouth and crunches down on the beads. A small black line trickles out the corner of her mouth and she uses the back of her wrist to wipe it away.

"Take it easy, babe." Jerry says.

"Mind your business." His girl responds coldly.

I stand up and shrug. I still feel like shit, but I have enough energy to get the hell out of this house of hostility, make it home, and rest.

"It is what it is." I move quickly to the door hoping the conversation is over with that saying. I need to get away from these two gunslingers and Katrina just ate two *freeing accelerates*. She calls out to me as I head towards the second floor steps and leans out the door. Four people are waiting at the bottom and move fanatically when they hear their dealers voice. In passing, I gawk at the guy I elbowed. He smiles at me as so the rest, all men with black lines like the cracks between a barren land etched on their face. Shifting eyes.

One takes a step towards me.

"Don't touch him!" Katrina shouts from her balcony and he listens.

What the hell?

"We're going to find it, Porkenstine!" She shouts and pulls another plant from her apron. "And with a smell like this," she runs the plant under her nose and exhales. "It won't be hard."

Shit. Leave it to mankind to destroy something precious.

CHAPTER THIRTEEN

Nightmare

I made an awful mistake. I feel like a parasite. No worse. A plague. To my mother, I'm a parasite. From the moment of my conception, I've drained the poor woman of her body and nutrients, then of her time and energy as I grew into a young man. She told me many times I was no easy baby, toddler or teen. Even up into my adulthood, too afraid to leave home and make my own path outside of my feeble dreams, I latched into her when I knew she needed a break as a caretaker to her crippled husband. When my dreams in music failed, that's when I did and completely stopped everything worth trying.

I have no education or desire to pick up basic work and as long as she says nothing, I do nothing besides sit my lazy ass down in my room and pick up her orders from Jerry. I'm a loser. I had the opportunity to save that man's life by just leaving him in the forest. Sure, he tried to kill me and that doesn't justify my actions of killing him, but I took something precious from him, exposed it to a doomed world, and corrupted it.

Sighing, I turn off my car and drop my keys into my jacket pocket. I've been gone for a while now. The kitchen lights are on, and I can see my mother through the sheer curtains standing over the sink and smoking a cigarette. Walking inside I'm hit with the most awful smell of fart combined with a bag of old coins. The back of my nose is set ablaze as I walk into the living room.

A quick glance at my dad, he's shaking harder than usual as if my mother didn't give him his night before and day medications. Thick beads of sweat cover the crown of his bald head and runs down the sides of his face. Upon seeing me walk past the television, his eyes grow wide, and his mouth opens slightly as if he wants to say something until the slam of the refrigerator door startles him to silence.

I hear Carol growl about something under her breath and lightly place my hand on her shoulder. She flinches and spins around.

"Thank, goodness." My mother washes her hands and dries them on a towel stained with brown blotches. "Got something for me?"

I raise an eyebrow. "No. You wanted me to get something up from the store?"

"Fuck. Jerry didn't give you a bag?"

I shake my head no. I don't think he cared enough to remember her order if she made one. Plus, he was too busy trying to get the location to the garden. Either way, after looking into my mother's eyes, she didn't need the bag. They weren't moving like a rattle-thank God, but her brown irises were shifting between myself and the kitchen door constantly.

I look over my shoulder and see Roger poking his head into

the space and holding tight onto his chair's wheels. He looks hesitant. Like a nervous puppy.

"Give me a minute!" My mother snaps.

On the stove, the lid to a large steel pot is clanking against the rim. She grabs a bowl from the cabinet, uses a pair of prongs to dig out a chunk of mushy green shit, and drops it into the dish. "I didn't cook any meat with it. Shouldn't be a problem."

I recoil with flared nostrils at the sight of overcooked, unseasoned cabbage stew and a cup of tap water in a glass coated with finger prints as the beverage. So much for presentation. There's not a drop of love in this meal.

My mother mumbles something underneath her breath as she gathers Roger's pills and whips them like dice in a small paper cup.

"Can you go back over there and grab a bag for me?"

"What! No. Ma, you need a break." I gently take the dish tray and slide it over to myself. Not only am I extremely exhausted, I'm not going to drive back to two extremely hostile people that have guns. I can feel the cold steel against the back of my head as I lead them to the garden. "Why don't you go lay down for a bit."

Carol sighs and keeps her head lowered. Her eyes are moving from side to side but not in a rattle and her hand is tapping on the edge of the sink. God, please whatever it is that I released in the world, don't let it take my mother.

I walk in the living room and set the tray down on the stand. Roger peeks into the kitchen probably wondering why his wife is standing, just gazing out into the space before her. It's actually the first time in a while I'm witnessing his focus off of the television. I too wonder what she's thinking about as I wheel my father to his shit smelling meal and place his medicine cup closer in reach.

The old man annoys me, but as my father I feel a twinge of sorrow for him. He sighs deeply, looks down at his food, then at me with watery eyes. I can't bear to see Roger like this, in such a sad state as if he's a little boy who lost their pet. He treated my mother like shit throughout the years and looking into his eyes, I sense that he's starting to feel regretful for his attitude towards her. Even I'm a bit concerned in her shift. The meal and her swearing at him is not like her. It's as though she's reached her breaking point.

What am I going to do? I can't go back to Jerry's, if weed is what will calm her down.

My keys jingle and the front door slams.

"Shit." I dash out of the house, but don't make it in time. My mother peels out of the driveway and pushes the accelerator. It's been four years since she drove a car and my aging vehicle cranks when she disappears around the corner, screeching against asphalt.

The headache from earlier I thought had faded returns with a hard knock behind my eyes. I wince and press my wrist on the bridge of my nose, anything to alleviate that pain, yet it beats harder.

I steal two of Roger's pain killers and quickly make him a peanut butter and jelly sandwich with a glass of milk in a clean cup. One mouth full of my mother's slop and he damn near threw up and seeing my meal made a faint light I thought I'd never see in his eye, turn on.

I fall onto the sofa beside him and take in a whiff of the strong odor, like a bag of wet old pennies.

"What the hell is that smell?"

"Gene." My dad moans. "Please bandage up this wound for me?"

My body aches as I sit up and search for him for the wound he's talking about. The closer I get to him, the stronger the smell becomes. I raise his shorts and gag. A large gash as if someone slashed him deep from one side of his thigh to the other is crusted with clotted blood. Fortunately, my father is paralyzed from the waist down, so I'm assuming he didn't feel a thing, but Christ!

His hands are quaking against his stomach, and he closes his eyes to trap tears, yet sadly some slip through. Without saying anything, I quickly rush to the bathroom and gather the first aid kit to dress his wound. We don't have a lot of medical supplies and everything in the box is past expiration date.

I take out the gauze, old peroxide, and large bandages. He needs to go to the hospital for stitches, but Carol took off with my car. Not to mention with the high dosage of prescribed medication, I'm starting to drift away into dreamland. I do my best and lay down like a tick on a dog once I'm done. Leeching and useless.

"How...did that...happen?" I say. The pain in my chest is gone, but now the weight of a grown human now sits on me and not in the way that I want. "You fell?"

Roger doesn't answer. I open one eye and look at him. The sandwich and milk are gone and he's picking at the mush in a daze. What the hell happened to him? Even when he came back from the war, disabled with no chance for a medical recovery outside of a miracle, and had to fully depend on his wife and I, my father still had some fight in his demeanor. I can't imagine my mother cutting him like that, from one end of the thigh to the other.

No.

He would've fought back. At least threw a punch at her.

But I've never seen Carol violent. Frustrated, yet never reaching physical aggression.

I force myself up and move to my bedroom. I hate to see the old man in such a pathetic state and truth be told, without work, I'm bound to become just like him. Nothing feels worth working for other than the garden. When I'm there, I feel great, alive and one with the nature as if I reconnected with it. Here, the world is shifting underneath my feet, and my body feels so heavy, drained, and crippling that I could crumble into a million pieces and die. Something tells me once I come down from this medicated high, the aches will be waiting for me like a person waiting for the return of their loaned money.

****

"Yulisi! Yulisi!"

A scream so strong I can hear the burn in their cracking throat stirs me awake. My eyes, fused with a thick coat of crust, break apart as I slowly open them.

I gasp and see through the darkness bathed in a full moons glow that I'm back in the garden deep in the pond, and leaning over onto the edge of earth. The woman continues to scream and call out to someone. My vision and sense of self are fuzzy. How the hell did I get here? I raise my head and squint my eyes There's a solemn aura that has engulfed the entire land. The dimness, a woman screaming, and birds *cawing*. Not their warming hellos but dying cries.

This can't be the garden.

I grip the earth and try to pull myself up, but a shocking pain travels from the tips of my toes to the crown of my head, making sure to bolt my four limbs on the way up and linger behind my eyes.

I holler and release myself back unto the water, in hopes

113

it's healing effects would take hold of me. My hands are covered in liver spots and wrinkles. Loose transparent skin hangs off my knobby fingers and my veins poke out like unearthed roots of ancient trees. When another cry slips from my throat, my voice is weak and frail.

"Oh God." I search for a glimpse of my reflection in the pond and catch it beside the copy of the moon. My jaw drops, eyes grow agape, and I shout at the old man staring back at me. I feel the aches of his joints and confusion that only comes when you reach the golden years of life. Sinking full-body in the pond doesn't help. If anything, it makes my discomfort worse. I try to climb out, but I feel like I weigh a ton. Too weak for myself and wet clothes, yet instinct tells me to get out to help whoever is screaming.

The cries from the woman and the animals grow louder. I pull with every ounce of my strength to get out of the water. A stone large and set deep enough in the ground serves me as an anchor and I drag my body across the damp earth. Cackling echoes and the sound of crunching stirs all around me. Exhausted, I raise my head and narrow my eyes to fix my sight to see what's happening. A bird lands with a hard thud beside me. Five more drop like flies from the trees down into the water. A woman on the other side holds the head of a dead swan to her chest and cries out to its mate floating in the pond, motionless.

Oh, God. The trees.

The eyes on the barks that once gazed down on me with speculation are now rattling.

"Yulisi!"

The woman. Nancy!

I reach out to her. She screams and extends her withered arm my way and calls out that name. I look behind me. Three women who've I never seen before, Katrina, and the male that attacked me, stand in the shallow water, all grinning. It's as if they crawled from the pond behind me without making a sound. Their eyes are bulbous, glowing red with black substance running from the corners of their mouth.

They leap out of the water and start clawing into the soil's natural veins, rip up the vegetation and spit black tar into the holes. I lift my upper body but flip back down like a dead fish. I can't move anymore, breathing is hard, and my sight is fading in and out. What have I done? I drop my head down on the dry grass and weep.

"*Yulisi!*" Nancy's cry tears my heart to pieces. All I ever wanted was to simply touch her.

I look up once more and come face to face with the wolf. His mouth, quivering and teeth dripping blood.

"You led them here." He snarls and snaps at my face.

CHAPTER FOURTEEN

Corruption

I wake up coated in sweat and gag at the scent and gooeyness of my own shit and piss being mashed between my butt and bedding. As I try to pull my blanket off, I have trouble taming my shaking hands and notice the number of little brown dots have increased along with the pain. From my fingers up to my elbows, they're coated with aged spots. What little hair I had left on my head is sprayed all over my pillow and the pain returned with intensity. Raising my arm feels as if someone hit me many times with a steel bat.

I can't move.

Every vein in my body is on fire.

My bones and joints are cracking with each turn, bend, and flex and my back aches when I attempt to straighten my posture.

"MOM!"

There's no answer. I holler out to her again and sit up, but she doesn't come, and my body screams again in agony.

I sniff down a knot forming in my throat and lay flat on

my back. As long as I don't move, I won't suffer. Part of me is begging myself to keep it cool. I am a grown man after all, but my other sense of self is stronger. The human side that is crying out for assistance, for someone to carry me in their warm arms to a bathtub full of boiling water and maybe bubbles to ease my whirlwind of a mind. I whimper and let the fountain of tears flow down the sides of my face as I keep my stiff arms at my sides. I'm disgusting.

Aint nothing like being drawn back to the day I was born. Sitting in my own fecal matter, in pain, and bawling.

Where is my mother to help me? Does she hear my cries from the kitchen, and will she come to help me to the bathroom, but after five minutes of calling her, she doesn't show up.

I turn my gaze out the window. It's still dark outside and the clock reads three fifteen and the space under my closed bedroom door is black. Not even the faint glow from the television that travels to my bedroom is here to comfort me.

Scouring in disgust, I roll out of bed, yell loudly when I land on the floor and crawl on my hands and knees outside where I'm hit with an even stronger smell. Metal. The same scent I got from Roger's wound. I call out to him, but no answer. Not a single light is on except for a morsel shimmering from the television and silence. No one is snoring and the only one breathing is me.

"Hello." I whisper through the eerie quietness. I'm scared, but there's nothing I can do in this condition. I move to the bathroom, turn the faucet onto the hottest level that it can go, and lay in the bowl like a plucked chicken getting prepped for the fire. If my body could scream hallelujah, it would. Instead, the scorching water relaxes my stomach. A bubble rises up my esophagus and I release a belch and a fart.

I clean myself off, drain the brown water from the tub and refill it with fresh warmer water with a small scoop of pink salt my mother keeps under the sink. She says it helps the skin leak out more toxins under the dermis. I'll take her word for it. It's not even close to being practically regenerative like the garden's pond, but it's the next best thing.

The telephone rings seven times in the kitchen. I let it and drop my head under water to reflect on my next moves.

I've made up my mind. This will be my last night in this house and seen in this town, hell, the world. I'm disappearing for good to the forest with Nancy whether the wolf likes it or not. It's been two days. Her lover, husband, whoever the fuck he was to her isn't coming back and I feel as if I'm connected to the land now. I ate from there. I bathed in the water. Being apart from it for too long brings me in the brink of death. And besides, here I'm a loser. There's no job that will take a man who hasn't worked a day in his entire fucking life, and I can't live with being an added burden to my mother.

Nancy will take care of me. I know she will.

I'm changing into a fresh pair of clothes when the phone rings again. My eyebrows rise and I stand still for a long minute as the bell continues to toll waiting for more noise to follow it. Roger would be shouting for mom to answer the call. I peek out the window and see my car is back in the driveway parked crooked.

"Dad." I call out. The phone stops ringing and I head straight to the living room to find him in his usual place-resting on the sofa, his blanket pulled up to the crown of his head. The television is on, but knocked down from its stand, his dinner table is along with the dishes I set earlier, is scattered across the living room.

My heart skips a beat, and I throw my hand over my mouth to stop bile from coming up. The smell of blood is powerful and there's a small brown stain on the cover that's placed over his head. "Dad?"

I reach down and rock him. He doesn't move. I stand and watch his body through the faint light of the television for a raise in his torso, yet he's stiff. Pulling down the cover and examining him will confirm what I suspect, but I don't want that. I can't stop shaking. Broken voiced, I call out to him again and he doesn't respond. With my hand against his cheek, I feel that his body is cold.

My father is dead.

I tug the sheet an inch lower and gag at the sight of a massive hole on the side of his head. His skull and brain are splattered all over his pillow and his tongue is hanging outside of his mouth. He was battered to death.

"Dad, I-

I drop my face into my hands, weep, and pray that he didn't feel a thing or see whatever struck him coming. I hope he was heavily medicated. I should've been awake to protect him.

I'm a worthless, piece of shit for a son that failed at everything.

I didn't hear anything. I didn't help him.

"I'm so sorry." I whisper.

A thought comes across my mind. I have to call the ambulance or the police. Someone! But what if they think I did this to Roger? I shouldn't be worrying. All I have to do is tell them the truth. My prints aren't on the weapon. There's no blood on me.

There was blood on that rock. Did I do it? I killed someone before. I could've been sleepwalking just moments ago.

What am I thinking?

I sprint to the kitchen and stop cold. My mother is standing in the corner, hidden in the darkness and laughs when she sees me clutching my hammering chest and pressed against the counter. She lowers her head and whispers something uncomprehending to herself with hands behind her back and rocking from side to side.

She's not right. I've never been the type to listen to my gut feelings-that I should've done the moment I ran over the guy-but something is telling me to back away from her. Something deep and buzzing under my skin. I can't though. Her toothy smile flashes before my eyes, what was once a beautiful sight I took for granted is now gone from my doing. The same dread I felt around Katrina and her buyer is now clinging to her like a second skin.

My hand reaches out for her. "Mom?"

The telephone rings and I look towards it hanging on the wall. A sharp, heavy object suddenly slams down on my hand.

"Fuck!" Christ. The fucking pain is staggering. I hold my burning wrist against my chest and lean over in agony.

"Useless little shit." Carol growls. I look up at my mother with tears in my eyes. She has a hammer raised high over her head. *Move!*

I swiftly duck and miss the swing. The iron head slams against the aged counter and breaks a chunk of it off.

My mother cackles and chases me around the kitchen into the living room and back to where we started, waving the hammer, hitting everything and anything in the way while trying to aim for me.

"Mom," I cry. She swings, misses again, and hits the steel pot of mush. It falls and spills all over the floor.

I lean against the sink and with my functioning hand, I search the rack of clean dishes for anything with a handle. "Please, STOP."

My mother's eyes are rattling, and her black-drool covered jaw is contorting. My heart sinks as the face that once was bright in her youth and beautiful in old age is gone. Now pale and distorted into rage.

She raises the hammer, and I jam a meat cutting knife directly in the center of her throat. She chokes and spits something black out at me. I gaze into her eyes as her expanding pupil takes over the faint blueness of her irises and feel the sudden strike of the hammer coming down on my right shoulder. We both fall over, and I scream in agony.

My heart. It hurts. I'm dying. My mother. My dad. My parents are gone because of me.

"God! Please," I weep. "I...can't do this...anymore." My heart is exploding, and my brain is melting. I just want to die.

The telephone rings once more. I clench my jaw, growl, and help myself up by grabbing onto the edge of the counter with pure rage and adrenaline.

Snatching the phone from the receiver, I snarl, "Who the *fuck* is this!"

A woman cackles on the other end and there's faint moaning in the background.

"Thanks for showing us the way."

I gasp. Katrina. Something *pops* and she laughs.

"I'll meet you there." *Click.*

My body burns with physical pain and rage. Fucking Katrina. That was a gunshot I heard on the phone and sure as shit that was Jerry probably clinging onto life before she took him out completely.

I have to get to the garden.

I wince in pain as I search for my car keys on the dining table and counter. Carol was the last person in my car. I cry as I search her pockets. Blood is oozing through the skin around the blade and that black tar-like substance drips from the corner of her mouth. Her body twitches at my touch but doesn't stir anymore. I pull my keys from her pocket and lean against the cabinet. I'm so sorry for being a shit son. To both of my parents. I'll never see them again.

I want to die, but I refuse to go out. Not now.

I kiss my parents goodbye, grab Carol's lighter and dash out the door. The pain of withering is at full-force but not stronger than the anger I have towards myself and Katrina. She's not going anywhere near that garden. No one is.

Going 95 through town, I blow past every stoplight. My vision is getting blurry. Either the shock and adrenaline are wearing down or I'm suffering the repercussions of being without that plant, pure fruit and pond water. I have to hold on. I'm not that far.

In my rear view mirror, red and blue lights flash. I push my foot down in the accelerator and make a sharp turn onto the back roads.

The cop is tight on my ass. I hear him command through the bullhorn that I pull over, but I'm not stopping for shit. I go as fast as possible with a strong sense of where I need to stop. It's too dark to see my marker anyways but there's a cord attached to my heart, reeling me in like a fish. I slam on the brakes and turn the wheel, hooking my car and avoiding a collision. Five cars are parked in the middle of the road at the entrance of the path.

"Shit." I quickly grab the gasoline from the trunk.

"Freeze. GET ON THE FUCKING GROUND." The cop

demands.

I can't see his face. The lights on his car are too bright. I also don't want to take the chance trying to search his eyes. I can only see his shadow perched over his door. He's got his gun pointed at me and shoots.

The bullet strikes my already wounded shoulder. I nearly stumble from the bullets push-back but regain my stance, quickly. Hell no. I didn't get this far for nothing.

I take off into the dark woods, dashing in a zig-zag, hearing the wisp of more metal speeding past my ear.

I released something awful into the world that makes people murderous. I've seen zombie movies and heard enough plague tales to know that shit will spread. The weeds. I have to burn them. I have to burn the entire fucking forest down. They're here. I can hear them cackling all around me. Even up above.

Spots clear of leaves allow the moon's glow to shine through. I run as fast as I can, hearing footsteps behind me. When I look over my shoulder and see three rays of search lights waving around in search of me. Christ, the cop called backup. A bright light from above shoots down before me and the trees dance in a frenzy under a helicopters winds.

"Dammit!"

There are people in here dashing around, climbing up the wooden legs like monkeys, leaping from branch to branch. My heart is slamming against my burning chest, and my knees are buckling under my weight. I can't run anymore, yet the hedge is right before me.

I pry the gas can open with my teeth and spray everything with gasoline. There's six gallons I empty out. I tear a piece of my shirt and douse it as well and set it ablaze with Carol's lighter.

"Gene." Katrina sings. Her face lights up at the sight of the rising flames, but only for a moment, she turns her bloodshot rattled gaze towards me and throws the wolf head at me. "A gift." She laughs.

I fall to the ground in massive chest pain. She climbs on top of me and holds my head still to face her. She then opens her mouth and digs her fingers into mine, separating my jaw from my upper teeth.

God, I'm in so much pain. So exhausted. I can't fight anymore. It's hot and hard to breathe through the smoke. People are cackling, men are hollering. I hear *pop! Pop! Pop!* "Get back!"

Katrina vomits black sweet tasting goo into my mouth and shoves her hand over my lips to ensure I don't spit it out. Why would I? I'm so tired of fighting against the corruption I bought from the garden. Humans couldn't handle the first one. Why would our creator bring something in this world so precious when he knows how disturbed we are? The slightest bit of light can easily be consumed.

My tongue swishes through the thick substance and picks up on little crunchy beads. It tastes like honey, gently slips down my throat, and warms my entire body from the inside out. The fire, consuming at first full of anger, suddenly smiles back at me. Bark embers fall onto me and burn my skin, however, it doesn't hurt. It tickles. I smile, feeling my strength return. The garden. It has the best soil for the beads brewing inside of me. I need to spread more. The others need to feel this bliss and be free. The woman on the other side. I will have her flesh whether she wants it or not. I will tear it from her bones and wrap it around my neck like a scarf.

I crawl to the pond and reach inside for the rock.

POP! POP!

The bullets in my back sting and I lose all feeling and control in my legs.

Like father, like son.

As beautiful darkness surrounds me, I rest my head on the ground and accept that hell is better than the life I once had.

Thank you for reading. Get ready for the long journey ahead

and check out the lore website for the manga, content not in

the novel, and upcoming hybrid arc of the saga, *Amongst*

Gods at `https://celestaraarchvies.com`